RADICAL RED

RADICAL RED

STORIES

Nathan Dixon

AMERICAN READER SERIES. NO. 43
BOA EDITIONS, LTD. * ROCHESTER, NY * 2025

Manufactured in the United States of America

First Edition
23 24 25 26 7 6 5 4 3 2 1

Publications by BOA Editions, Ltd.—a not-for-profit corporation under section 501 (c) (3) of the United States Internal Revenue Code—are made possible with funds from a variety of sources, including public funds from the Literature Program of the National Endowment for the Arts; the New York State Council on the Arts, a state agency; and the County of Monroe, NY. Private funding sources include the Max and Marian Farash Charitable Foundation; the Mary S. Mulligan Charitable Trust; the Rochester Area Community Foundation; the Ames-Amzalak Memorial Trust in memory of Henry Ames, Semon Amzalak, and Dan Amzalak; the LGBT Fund of Greater Rochester; and contributions from many individuals nationwide. See Colophon on page 206 for special individual acknowledgments.

Cover Art and Design: Sandy Knight
Interior Design and Composition: Isabella Madeira
BOA Logo: Mirko

BOA Editions books are available electronically through BookShare, an online distributor offering Large-Print, Braille, Multimedia Audio Book, and Dyslexic formats, as well as through e-readers that feature text to speech capabilities.

Cataloging-in-Publication Data is available from the Library of Congress.

BOA Editions, Ltd.
250 North Goodman Street, Suite 306
Rochester, NY 14607
www.boaeditions.org
A. Poulin, Jr., Founder (1938-1996)

I believe in an America where millions of Americans believe in an America that's the America millions of Americans believe in. That's the America I love.

—United States Senator and Candidate for President of the United States Mitt Romney

Contents

Unidentified Black Male

You start out in 1954 by saying, "Nigger, nigger, nigger." By 1968 you can't say "nigger"—that hurts you, backfires. So you say stuff like, uh, forced busing, states' rights, and all that stuff, and you're getting so abstract. Now you're talking about cutting taxes, and all these things you're talking about are totally economic things and a byproduct of them is, blacks get hurt worse than whites. . . . "We want to cut this," is much more abstract than even the busing thing, uh, and a hell of a lot more abstract than "Nigger, nigger."

—Consultant to United States Presidents Ronald Reagan and George H.W. Bush and Chairman of the Republican National Committee Lee Atwater

If we allow it to happen, then the city jungle will cease to be a metaphor. It will become a barbaric reality, and the brutal society that now flourishes in the core cities of America will annex the affluent suburbs.

—President of the United States Richard Nixon

The war on crime is a never-ending one. And it is necessary that we pursue it constantly and with vigor if our citizens are to be safe on our streets and in their homes.

—President of the United States Ronald Reagan

Many New York families . . . have had to give up the pleasure of a leisurely stroll in the Park at dusk, the Saturday visit to the playground with their families, the bike ride at dawn, or just sitting on their stoops—given them up as hostages to a world ruled by the law of the streets, as roving bands of wild criminals roam our neighborhoods, dispensing their own vicious brand of twisted hatred on whomever they encounter. . . . [It is] a dangerously permissive atmosphere which allows criminals of every age to beat and rape a helpless woman and then laugh at her family's anguish . . . laugh because they know that soon, very soon, they will be returned to the streets to rape and maim and kill once again—and yet face no great personal risk to themselves.

. . . I am not looking to psychoanalyze or understand them, I am looking to punish them. . . . I want them to be afraid.

How can our great society tolerate the continued brutalization of its citizens by crazed misfits? Criminals must be told that their CIVIL LIBERTIES END WHEN AN ATTACK ON OUR SAFETY BEGINS!

. . . Let our politicians give back our police department's power to keep us safe. Unshackle them from the constant chant of "police brutality." . . . Give New York back to the citizens who have earned the right to be New Yorkers. . . . BRING BACK THE DEATH PENALTY AND BRING BACK OUR POLICE.

—President of the United States Donald Trump

1.

The police officer—a white man—walked over the crumbling asphalt that led to the sprawling brick tenements. Past liquor stores and payday loan lenders, past pawnshops and bodegas, neon words burning in barred windows. He was very pale in the sunlight and wore a dark blue uniform with a shining silver star on his chest. He whistled as he walked, a song he couldn't place. Something old and reminiscent of war. He had parked his car on the other side of the old railroad tracks where the grass was gray and grew waist high between the rusty steel bars that ran in both directions forever.

People cursed him under their breath as he passed. Old men in suits, tapping along with canes, old women in bright monochrome with feathers in their hats, young women with children flocked about their waists, young women pushing strollers along the cracked sidewalks, younger women, still, with books beneath their arms, their hair in tight braids, glasses perched upon their noses. They shook their heads, whispered to one another, clutched at their children as the police officer passed.

As he moved deeper into the complex of tenements, young men scattered before him as he whistled along his way. As he sucked at his pointed teeth and spat blood on the asphalt. Young men zipped up alleyways in pitter-patter shoes, their voices echoing down the shallow canyons. Five-O, Five-O, they called. Some ducked behind the plywood sheets nailed over the tenement doorways, others into corner stores that had trapdoors in the back. Heads peeked from second and third story windows, cars pulled away from corners. Away. The black and brown friends of the black boy took off in different directions. Like cockroaches when someone flips the overhead switch. That's what the police officer thought. Cockroaches in different directions so that you can never stomp them all out.

The black boy tried to run, but he wasn't as fast as his friends. The officer caught up to him quickly. Didn't have to lay a finger on him, because the black boy knew the drill, like all the other boys on this side of town. As soon as the officer was close enough, the boy found the nearest brick wall and made himself a starfish. The officer stood behind him, panting and coughing. He cleared his throat and spat as he stood up. Shouldn't make me run like that, he said.

The boy shook his head, staring at the dirty bricks in front of him, trying to catch his own breath. I didn't do nothing, he said, as the officer kicked his feet farther apart. I didn't do nothing, as the officer ran his hands up and down the boy's legs—I didn't do nothing—over his crotch, his stomach, under his arms. Same old, same old, the officer said. He reached into the boy's pockets and pulled out a key, some loose change, a few balls made of looped rubber bands.

What did you throw on the ground back there? he asked.

I didn't do nothing, the boy answered.

Before the words were out of his mouth, though, the officer had grabbed his shoulder and whipped him around so that they were standing face to face. The officer pushed him back against the wall, and the boy could feel the gritty bricks against the back of his head. He saw blood dripping from the officer's sharp teeth.

Open your mouth, the white man said.

What? the boy whispered, trying to catch his breath. He kept looking at the gun on the officer's belt. His grandmother had told him to always watch their hands.

Open it, the officer said, squeezing harder. Wider, the officer said.

The boy watched the rubber band balls bounce on the ground. Once, twice, three times, they rolled toward the gutter in a row. He thought they would all go down the storm drain. Plip-plop. But the last one stopped before it got there. Silly how it didn't go down like the others, he thought. That's so silly. The officer's hand was in his mouth, then it was pushing down his throat. He retched, but it was muffled by the arm reaching deeper, plugged by the arm, pushed down. How? he thought, squeezing closed his eyes, his jaw beginning to unhinge. How could this happen? Tears streamed down his face, his knees buckled, he started to fall. But the officer caught him by his throat and pinned him against the wall—his other hand grabbing at something inside the boy, his arm pushed in past the elbow now. The boy could feel the fingers clutching at something in his belly. Could feel something coming loose. Then—all of a sudden—pulled free. There was a slick wet sound, like water lurching from a spigot, almost a whistle, as the boy vomited the white man's arm.

When he opened his eyes again, he could see—through his tears—that the officer held something in his hand. The man's pink fingers were splayed, and there, in the pink palm, was the boy's voice, wiggling like a little slice of jello. It was about as big as the rubber band ball, and without thinking, the boy reached for it, not knowing what it was, but knowing it was his.

Before he could grab it, though, the officer punched him in the face. A flat smack that the boy heard before he felt.

Cupping his hands to his cheek, he watched as the officer shook his head at him—*no*—and slipped the voice into his pants pocket. Watched as the officer looked him up and down. Listened as the officer told him to undress. The boy couldn't understand. He kept his eyes on the gun as he tried to ask what he had done wrong. But no sound came out when he opened his mouth. He touched his lips, felt them moving, felt his jaw flapping up and down, his tongue curling to make words, but there were no sounds. He had no voice.

Again, the officer told him to undress. Go on and take your clothes off, he said. But the boy could only squint at him, his cheek beginning to swell where he had been hit. Again, his mouth moved but no words came out. He shook his head to tell the officer he wouldn't do it, his fingers still touching his lips.

I guess we'll do it the hard way, then, the officer said, spitting.

He turned his head to the side and spoke into the crackling black box on his shoulder. A series of numbers and letters, then the words: *unidentified black male, age twelve to fifteen*. Above him, tattered clouds floated very slowly in wisps through the blue sky from one building top to another. A static voice answered from the black box, scratching into the heavy quiet, and the officer nodded his head. Looked at the boy and raised his eyebrows.

Now, he said, you going to undress or not?

The boy moved his mouth in response, without sound, then shook his head again. No.

2.

Soon a squad of police cars came screaming from the distance, bouncing over the railroad tracks, over the crumbling asphalt. Screaming right up to the spot on the sidewalk where the black boy and the white officer stood. The sirens went silent as the car doors opened, but the blue and red lights kept swinging around. The officers leapt out with their guns pointed toward the boy, all of them shouting as they crouched behind their car doors. Shielding themselves from the youth who stood perfectly still with his hands in his mouth.

He could smell them as he pulled off his jacket. Sweaty bodies. As he pulled off his T-shirt and dropped it on the ground. Screaming red faces, they advanced in their bulletproof vests. Navy blue fatigues, bright stars, sour sweat. He could taste them almost, as they stepped closer, pushed the noses of their guns toward his chest.

Slowly, they kept saying. Easy now, do it slowly, the red and blue lights flashing on their faces, into their hollow mouths. Sharp teeth. They snapped like dogs. Shoes, they said. So he stepped from his shoes. Slowly, they said. Now your pants.

He unbuckled his belt with one hand, his pants sagging off his hips, the other hand still raised high in the air. Behind the officers, he could see his friends peeking at him from an alleyway. He opened his mouth to call out to them, to ask them to go get help. But one of the officers reached out and grabbed his pants and pulled them down.

His boxer shorts came down with them, and the boy tried to snatch them up again. But the one who had pulled them down said, No. All the others behind him said, No. One screamed, Stop resisting. Put your hands on your head. He felt the cold tip of a pistol on his chest, pushing him back against the brick. Suddenly he felt nauseous again, remembering the officer's arm down his throat.

Naked, shivering, small against the backdrop of the red brick wall, he watched their fingers tickle the triggers.

He flinched when they touched him. Jerking this way and that, scrunching up in anticipation. The officers laughed at him as he danced.

After a while they handcuffed him and sat him on the street curb. They asked him where he lived and what he was doing. Told him if he didn't cooperate there would be more trouble. But he couldn't answer because his voice was in the first officer's pocket.

They told him they were confiscating his clothes because they were bought with drug money. His home would be seized too if he didn't cooperate. No matter who's in it, they said. If you live there, we'll take it. That's the law. They said everything would be easier if he helped them. That he could be a good guy for once. That his family would be proud of him. For once.

Staring at their shiny black shoes, he felt the grit from the curb digging into his skin, his bare buttocks on the little swell of cracked concrete.

They put him in the back of a patrol car, told him he better not piss himself, and slammed the door shut. As they pulled away, more police cars sped into the canyon-land of brick tenements. Beneath the blue sky with the tattered clouds strafing from building top to building top, the calls of Five-O ringing out in the street.

3.

There were other naked boys in the holding cell. It was very dark, and they were kept there for a very long time. Almost all of them were black boys or brown boys, and none of them talked to each other. The boy wondered if any of them could talk. It seemed unlikely. There were a few tatted-up, bald-headed white boys, but they kept to themselves in the corner and mouthed threats and sneered whenever a black or brown boy passed too close. On a few occasions, regular white boys were ushered in wearing their clothes. They clutched the metal bars, looked over their shoulders at the naked black and brown boys, and quietly cried to themselves. They were the only ones who could make any noise, and after a little while, they were ushered out again.

There was no way to tell the time, no window to see the sun. Sometimes an officer walked down the hallway, running his baton along the bars of the cell. Ping, ping, ping, ping. But even this was irregular. They ate from hard plastic trays that were passed one by one through the mail slot. The black boy found it impossible to eat from the tray and cover himself at the same time. On his first day, as he was trying to figure out what to do, a bigger boy hit him in the face and took his food. All the others laughed and laughed—silently—holding their bellies. After that, he ate as quickly as he could.

The bathroom was a plastic bucket in the corner opposite the tatted-up, bald-headed white gang. Nobody had very good aim. The boys tiptoed through the filth and squatted when they had to go. Tried to keep from retching as they squirmed atop the bucket. There was nothing to wipe with afterward but chips of concrete on the floor.

As more and more boys crowded into the cell, little cliques and cadres developed. Lots of the boys seemed to know exactly what they were doing. They bought and sold things from one another, pulled plastic pouches from their assholes. Smoked and drank in the corners, laughed silently to each other. They communicated with a variety of hand and body gestures, but never when the guards came pinging past.

One day there were oranges on the lunch tray and a very pretty, light-skinned boy who was popular with all the cliques tried to juggle to entertain his friends. He dropped all three oranges in a row, and they rolled over to the black boy who picked them up and juggled them all with a single hand. The other boys began laughing silently and cheering with their arms. They threw more and more oranges at the boy until he was juggling nine of them, then twelve, then fifteen. Bouncing them off the ceiling and the walls. It looked like he had twenty hands. All the boys went wild. The light-skinned boy offered to teach the black boy the secret sign language in return for juggling lessons. But the leader of one of the gangs didn't like this and stabbed the pretty boy in the neck. When the guards came the next day and dragged him out by his feet, his head bumped along the ground. He left a slick trail of blood.

At night—when they thought it was night—all the little boys moved to the walls of the cell and tried to sleep with their bare backs against the concrete there. It was always very cold, and no one slept for very long. Some boys cried silently, sniffling on the floor, and others told them to shut up by kicking their heads. Many of the boys huddled together with their friends against the walls, clutching at one another as if they might sink through the floor.

4.

One day they were all given clothes that were much too big for them—men's clothes—and led from the cell one by one. Down a concrete hallway that smelled like mildew and glowed green in the muddled light. To a room with a metal table bolted to the ground and a light bulb hanging in a cage. Behind the table was a white man who was losing his hair. He wore heavy-framed glasses with cracked lenses and a wrinkled suit stained with coffee. Coffee dribbled from the sides of his mouth as he gulped it down between heavy breaths. He constantly pulled at what little hair he had left and told all the boys they must plea.

You better plea, he told the black boy, looking at the sheet of paper on the metal table. They're giving you a good deal here, he said, glancing up. No jail time. You can go right back home. Really. This is a no brainer, he said, running a hand through his flat brown hair, pulling it out in fistfuls. Laying limp strands on the table beside his coffee mug.

The boy tried to say he didn't do anything wrong. That his friends might have done something—he didn't know—but he didn't do anything. He promised, he tried to say. He was just walking home from school.

But nothing came out. No matter how hard he tried, he couldn't make a sound. He pounded his palms on the table. Nothing. He balled his hands into fists, shook them in the air above his head. Nothing.

Otherwise, you could get a couple of years, said the man on the other side of the table. Minimum sentences, you know. A couple of years. He took a big swig of coffee and stared at the paper until the boy calmed down. Yes, he said, you better plea, it's the smart thing to do. When it's over, you can go right back home.

5.

After the talk, the boy sat in the hallway with all the other boys. Crouched in their baggy clothes, waiting to talk to the coffee-drinker. In front of them, an officer paced back and forth with an assault rifle in his hands, whistling a song that sounded very old. And very happy. The boy remembered the rubber band balls bouncing on the asphalt in the sunshine. Down the drain, plip-plop. The one stopping just in front of the metal grate in the gutter. How silly.

Once everyone had seen the man with the cracked glasses, they all marched up the stairway at the end of the hall. Their footsteps echoed loud and hollow, none of them in perfect time. Like old-timey pickaxes hitting the ground in a row, clop-clop, clop-clop. Laying down a railroad track. Soft shoes against gray metal, the police officers telling them to hurry up, to keep together. It will all be over soon, they said, tapping their assault rifles. Up they marched—clop-clop, clop-clop—each looking at the baggy pants of the boy in front of him.

Once, when the black boy looked up, he saw the stairs went on forever, the zigzags circling round and round in the green light. He suddenly couldn't tell if he was looking up or down and got very dizzy and started missing steps. But before he fell, an officer grabbed the back of his head and forced it forward so that he was again staring at the legs of the boy in front of him. He wanted to thank the officer for that. But, of course, he didn't have a voice.

There were doors after each set of stairs, and, after a while, the officer in front opened one of them. Held it open for the boys to walk through—into a hallway that was painted yellow and had a long wooden bench, like a church pew, along the wall. They all sat down. Then, another officer with an assault rifle pulled them from their seats—one by one—and led them through a swinging door. When it was the boy's turn, he stood up like the others before him and walked through the door. Into a room with wooden walls. He stood behind a table with the rumple-suited man in the cracked glasses. Coffee dribbled from the man's mouth as he grimaced and pulled out his hair.

Up front was a judge in a black gown. He was white. Very tan, very bald, his body looked like it was poured from concrete. He slurped at a hollowed-out pineapple with a pink paper umbrella stuck into the top. When he yawned, he looked up at the ceiling and smiled and shook his head. As if he and God had a running joke. When he banged his hammer the lights in the courtroom flickered and the boy could see nothing but the judge's electric green skeleton shining through his skin. Neon bright, buzzing and crackling in the dark. The rictus of a reaper, cackling on the bench. His hammer looked like a swinging blade.

No one else seemed to notice when the lights flickered, and the boy started wondering if the bailiff might come and pull out his eyes as well and lock them away with his voice.

On the other side of the aisle—opposite the black boy and the man in the rumpled suit—was a large man who seemed to be in charge. He too was white, and the judge called him the prosecutor. He towered above everyone else in his crisp gray suit and had a clean-shaven face and purple bags under his eyes. Every few minutes he picked up a silver-handled mirror to make sure his hair was in place.

This man frowned and shook his head as the boy stumbled up to the stand.

I already regret doing this, he said, but let's see what you have to say.

A little old lady at a typewriter began clicking away as the prosecutor opened his briefcase. Voices of all shapes and sizes spilled out onto the table. Little jello globs, pink, green and orange, bright purple and blue, bouncing from the table to the floor, squeaking and burbling and shouting. I didn't do nothing.

Goddamn it! shouted the judge, banging his gavel. Goddamn it! Order in the court. The lights flicked on and off in time with the gavel. A strange morse code. Kapow. Pow, pow. The judge's skeleton danced an electric jig on the bench. He swung the hammer-blade like he was stabbing someone.

The bailiff and the prosecutor's assistants collected the squirming voices. The boy's public defender even lent a hand, chasing after a yellow voice wailing down the aisle. My children, it kept saying. What about my children?

Once they were secure again in the briefcase, the prosecutor walked to the stand, and told the boy to open his mouth.

The boy looked up at the judge who was slurping at his pineapple cup. There appeared to be someone under the desk sucking him off. When the judge realized the boy was looking at him, he banged his gavel. His fizzing, razzle-dazzle skull nodded up and down.

Obediently, the boy swallowed his voice. And once he found that he could speak, he started jabbering away, excited. I wasn't doing nothing, he said. Nothing, just walking home from school when this cop rolled up, and I didn't have anything on me. I don't even mess with that stuff. I tried to tell him it wasn't me. That I don't even know—I tried to tell him—

But the judge banged his hammer—pow! pow! pow! Order in the court, he said. Beneath the judge's bench, the blonde head bobbed up and down.

We don't care what happened, the prosecutor said. You've already pleaded guilty. The public defender stood up and nodded his head vigorously. Yes sir, he shouted. Yes sir.

We'll let you go now, the prosecutor continued. If you tell us what you told us you would tell us.

The boy swore everything that he said was the truth and told them everything he knew. Then more. He didn't know much, he said. Didn't know the drug dealers. Not personally. Just who they were. Which corners they stood on, their names, that's all. When he was done, he started making things up so that the prosecutor wouldn't take his voice again.

Is that all? the prosecutor kept asking. You can't give us anything else?

The boy kept talking, swore all of it was true. He started sweating as the prosecutor shook his head. As the judge started shaking his head. Then finished off whatever was in the pineapple cup.

The boy was ashamed he didn't know any more. He had disappointed everyone and couldn't look them in the face. The rumple-suited man nodded at him from behind the table, his eyes wide behind his cracked glasses. He moved his hand like a rolling wheel as if to hurry him along.

And—um—there's Freemont and MLK, the boy said. I've seen some of them up there. He rocked back and forth as he stared at the wooden banister in front of him. I think there's—um—I think there's—

That's enough, the prosecutor said, rolling up his sleeve. He flexed his fingers, made his hand into a fist, then opened it wide again.

The boy leaned back in the chair as if to get away from him, but there was nowhere to go. He knew what he was supposed to do, and he opened his mouth. He didn't want to get beat up again. He felt the hand reach down his throat, all the way to the elbow, felt his voice jiggling loose. Again, he heard the slick wet sound, though this time it didn't hurt as much.

Through his tears, he watched the prosecutor walk back to the table and drop his voice into his briefcase among the others, then slam the briefcase closed. You're free to go, he said, staring at himself in his silver mirror.

The judge banged his hammer again. Voltaic bones rattling, tripping the light fantastic. Beneath the bench, the blonde woman cooed between the gagging wet sounds.

The boy stood up and walked away.

6.

Free, they said. Free. The officer led him to a little window in the hallway with a heavy black woman behind it and told him when he was done, he could go. The woman gave him a bill. It was longer than his arm and hard to understand. He pointed to it and shrugged his shoulders. She took it from his hands and began reading. About how he owed them money for staying in their jail, for eating their food, for wearing their clothes. About how he owed the police officers for arresting him and the little rumple-suited man for pleading him. About how he owed the prosecutor for prosecuting him and the judge for judging him and the parole officer for paroling him. Or else, the heavy woman said, you'll have to come back to jail.

He shook his head at her, confused. Tried to argue. He had never asked for any of those things. He was just a kid. He didn't have any money.

But she wouldn't even look at him. That's the price, she said, circling it with her red marker. And that's the due date there. Also, if you ever want to vote, she said, you'll have to pay for that too. That's separate.

Handing back the long receipt, she called out, NEXT, and looked behind the boy to the long line of boys. They shuffled across the tile toward the woman as if they were still shackled. With no voice to argue, the boy shoved the receipt into his pocket and walked in his baggy clothes to the elevator. Inside of it were two police officers, one punching buttons on the wall. The other one shook his head at the boy.

I'm sorry, son, he said. You'll have to take the stairs. The first officer laughed, his sharp teeth clapping together. Covered in blood.

Clop-clop, clop-clop, all alone in the muddled green light, down the zigzags, round and round until he found the red EXIT letters.

Outside the day was very blue and everything seemed enormous. The receipt hung from his pocket, fluttered out behind him like a crinkly white tail. He walked away from the jail to the bus stop by the street and sat down on the bench, wondering how he would get home. He didn't have any money. And what about the money he owed? He wondered how he would pay the bill.

The same ragged clouds, like torn apart cotton balls, hung in the sky. Looking violent. It had been a long time since he had seen the sky, and he couldn't tell if the clouds were moving or if he himself was floating. When the bus came, the boy turned his pockets inside out, and the driver shook his head. He gave the boy a transit map, pointed his finger toward the horizon, and told him to walk.

Because the sun was so bright, the boy had to squint, and the baggy clothes weighed him down. He felt like he was wearing someone else's skin. The big woolly skin of some giant animal, his own body the bones beneath it. He imagined himself with an electric skeleton like the judge. Tingling all up and down his spine—zip-zap—his feet wanted to dance out in front of him. Free at last. Free at last. Thank God Almighty . . .

Everything was huge all around him as he careened out into the open. It was a long walk home, but he was determined to prance all the way. He wanted to sing to pass the time, to add cadence to his tip-tapping feet. Shaggy skin on electric bones, vibrating in the sunlight. But when he opened his mouth to sing, nothing came out.

He hung his head, and stared at the concrete, wondering how he would get the money. He beat out a rhythm with his palms on his thighs. He couldn't tell if the song was happy or sad.

7.

His grandmother told him not to tell anyone. They think you went to visit your cousins, she said. That's what I told them. And that's the truth. The only light in the room was the lamp on the end table beside her. It spotlighted the left side of her face, steep angles and bright smooth skin. She shook her head at him. A damn shame is what it is, she said. Just like your father.

The other side of her face was a dark outline. The lamp projected her shadow onto the opposite wall, a silhouette that seemed like it had been there forever. He looked at the silhouette instead of looking at her as she made her clucking sounds. People thinking we've got criminals in here, she said. You know they can take this house away, don't you? They already came around here once, talking about drugs. I don't know what you're up to, boy.

He tried to protest. Tried to tell her he hadn't done anything wrong. But, of course, he couldn't say a thing.

She walked across the room, flipped the light switch, and the overhead glared down. Suddenly, the boy remembered the light swinging in the cage above the rumple-suited man. Remembered the coffee dribbling from his mouth. His hair pulling loose in his hands.

Look at you, she said. Afraid of a little light. What'd they dress you up in anyway?

He looked down at himself and shrugged.

Those clothes are too big, she said. Looking over the tops of her glasses. Not meant for a boy, are they?

He shrugged again.

You look like your daddy. Shrunk down, shriveled up. She put her hand on her hip. What's wrong with you? she asked. Cat got your tongue? She took two steps over the rug in her slippers and put a hand on the back of his head. Come on, she said.

He shied away, but she kept her hand on his crown. Her voice was softer now. Cradling him.

Come on now and get your supper, she said. Leading him toward the kitchen. I know they hurt you. I know it. But you've got to be strong now. Be smart. Make sure they don't catch you again.

8.

He was afraid to leave the apartment. He spent as much time as he could in his bedroom. Practicing his juggling tricks and reading books about the Wild West. A long time ago, a relative of his had been in the circus and toured all over the country. A sideshow music man, his grandmother used to tell him. Her own daddy's brother, who brought around freaks when he came home from the road. Years ago, she had given the boy the old red and yellow posters to pin up in his bedroom. Baron Baloobo the One-Man Band. Singing Cowboy Songs from the Old Wild West. The Blue Shadow and his Music Machine. Brass Jazz from New Orleans. The Riverboat's Best. In between dime novels from the library sale, the boy practiced his quick draw with his old cap guns. He could juggle those as well. He practiced picking off the sheriff and his deputies. Practiced twirling them around his fingers, throwing them in the air, catching them behind his back before returning them to their holsters. His grandmother had warned him never to take the cap guns outside. You'll be dead before you're out the door, she said. Sometimes he wished he had a real one. But then he reconsidered. Down among his books and action figures, surrounded by the red and yellow posters, he wished he never had to leave at all.

Everything in the tenements seemed dark after that bright walk home from jail. All the corner boys called him *snitch* and told him he would *get his* when the time came. He figured they would come for him after dark and found himself wondering—even in the middle of the day—if the sun would suddenly blink off like a bulb.

He wore a hoodie when he went out so they wouldn't recognize him. And he hurried between the alleyways, stuck to the walls like an insect—scuttle, scuttle—knowing they could outrun him if they tried.

It wasn't just the corner boys, though, that he was hiding from. There were police officers too. They rode through the streets in Humvee tanks, all of them wearing camouflage, carrying assault rifles. It was worse now than it was when they had taken him away. He didn't know how much time had passed. It felt like years. And now, between the brick tenements, they waged their war in the open, rounding up everyone who didn't hide, everyone like him who wasn't fast enough.

They expelled him from school for missing too many days, and when he tried to explain, they wouldn't listen. They couldn't hear him. Shaking their heads, they called him a criminal, pushed him outside, told him not to come back.

He never told his grandma about that. Instead, he left the apartment every morning as if nothing had happened. A shadow between the buildings before the sun came up. Silently, off to the train tracks where the grass grew waist high and gray. Where neither the corner boys nor the police officers would look for him. Everything gray out there, even in the sunlight. Like there was a filter between himself and the sun.

9.

Before he got arrested, his grandma had tried to get him a job at the hair salon. But he hadn't wanted to work there because it was a job for girls. Now he went to the barbershop next door and tried to get a job sweeping up, but they told him they already had a boy for that. Come back in the summer, they told him. We might have a job then.

Afterward, he stood on the corner with the black men and the Mexicans who got picked up for construction jobs and yard work in the suburbs. These men smoked cigarettes and talked about old times, blowing great clouds into the greasy light. The Mexicans jabbered away in Spanish, but when they talked about women they used their hands, and the boy could understand their jokes.

The drivers, though, who came to pick them up said he was too small to work. A couple years yet, young blood, they said. You'll sprout up like a weed—put these old men to shame. A couple years yet, they said, driving away in their trucks.

He walked out to the train tracks in the mornings, to the rusty steel bars that ran in both directions forever. Away from the towering brick tenements. Away from the cops and the corner boys. He balanced along the rails in his hoodie, imagining he was a tightrope walker. A famous circus performer. Imagining the ground so far below him that one missed step might be his last. He pretended to twirl a mustache in his fingers. Pretended the muted sunlight was because of the big tent up above him. And when he teetered back and forth on one leg, he could almost hear the people cheering in the grandstands. Farther and farther every day, he sometimes strayed from the tracks to pick his way through abandoned strip malls and old factories with broken machines inside. He found dirty rubber bands and looped them into balls. Juggled like a clown with twenty arms.

He wondered what had happened to the other boys with whom he had shared the holding cell. He tried to remember how their faces had looked when he juggled all those oranges, but he could only recall the dead boy being dragged from the cell. A hole in his neck, his head bouncing on the ground. He remembered the pretty boy trying to tell him something, his mouth moving silently, his fingers making signs. As he hopped from rail to rail, he tried to teach himself to whistle like the officer with the assault rifle had done. He got a little closer every day.

His old friends were gone. One shot by a policeman and dead. One tagged in a drive-by and sent to his auntie in the country. One deported along with his mother and father, leaving behind his little sisters. One off to foster care, one in jail.

The world seemed bigger every day, and darker, and after a while he stopped trying to use his voice. Those first few days he had screamed and screamed, but he could never make a sound. He felt his mouth with his hands, inside and out, massaged his throat to make it work. But it was deeper, the officer had reached deeper, then the prosecutor—deeper—to pull it out. They had snatched it from his insides like it was nothing at all. Like they had done it a million times before. Rolling up their sleeves, taking deep breaths like they didn't really want to do it. But had to do it. Had to leave him hollow. Invisible. Silent.

He imagined a room behind the skeleton judge. A room full of jiggling jello voices. Bright, burbling, and happy, gushing and gossiping in a room with white walls that went on forever. He imagined himself a great ring-master conducting the chorus of globular colors. Doffing his top hat and cracking his whip before bringing them to a crescendo. Acrobatic voices tumbling through the air on trapezes, flipping and dipping, in time with his whip. Crack! A million voices bouncing and elastic—crack!—zipping back and forth in billowing rainbows. Dancing. Voices roaring and trumpeting, chasing one another in stacked harmonies. Crack. A great cacophony of sound—calling, responding, ripping open the air so that water ran from the cracked walls. A flood. Deafening voices ringing like bells, banging down the doors of the jailhouse. Free!

10.

He thought if he could raise the money he owed, maybe they would give him back his voice. Let him tiptoe into that white room and retrieve what belonged to him. That's what he told himself he was doing as he balanced his way down the rails. Looking for work, always looking for work. When he passed into town, he walked to the fast-food restaurants and the discount stores. To the retail outlets boasting half-price sales. The people were usually nice at first, giving him the job application, helping him fill it out. But whenever they came to the inevitable question their faces always puckered up. Have you been convicted of a felony? they asked, raising their eyebrows.

It got very quiet then, and the light would shift as he stared at the ground. He never answered at first, thinking they might move on. But they always waited, the quiet growing heavy and dark. And after a while he would nod—ashamed—and look up at them. Then it was their turn to look away. Lemon-faced, his answer always sour in their mouths.

Sometimes that was the end of it. They shrugged their shoulders and walked away. Other times, they finished their questions and told him they would get in touch if there was an opening. But there was never an opening.

It was like he had done something wrong—wanting work, asking for a job—and he always fled from the buildings with his hood over his head, trying to hide from everyone he saw. Trying to hide from the sun itself that seemed to fade day by day. His fault for being arrested, his fault for living where he lived, his fault for missing school, his fault for wanting work.

As he ran back toward the train tracks, the white folks on the sidewalks shied away. They raised their hands to protect themselves and pulled their children close. They locked their car doors and shouted the word *thug*. Some women screamed and pressed themselves flush against buildings. Breathless. They tore off their clothes and rubbed their crotches with their hands. Men pulled pistols from their hip pockets and blasted—willy-nilly—at the running boy. At the boy who ran and ran but never moved at all. At the boy who just kept shrinking into the darkling world.

He considered lying to the managers. Telling them he had never been to jail. But what was the point? He could see their glowing skeletons beneath their managerial khaki. They were all in cahoots. He imagined the police bursting through the doors as soon as he lied. Biting at his neck, chewing on his guts, a heap of rabid dogs. It was no good. He could see their sharpened teeth and became convinced that the job search would only lead him back to jail.

He couldn't think of any way to get the money. They had probably lost his voice anyway. Smothered it under the heap of melting voices in the white room. The walls closing in.

Every morning he wandered out to the railroad tracks, hustling from shadow to shadow, his hood pulled over his head, afraid someone might see him. Toward the steel bars of the railroad tracks where he could pretend to be someone else. Down in the gray grass, hiding in a hoodie. An unidentified black male, age twelve to fifteen. Juggling frantically through the fading world. Lost in a circus of make-believe. A criminal, trying to whistle an old sad song that he had heard from an officer's lips. Keep your balance. Down along the steel bars that ran in both directions forever. A criminal with bright colors and sound on his mind. A criminal, clapping rhythms down the rails.

The Doctor's Declarations

There must doubtless be an unhappy influence on the manners of our people produced by the existence of slavery among us. The whole commerce between master and slave is a perpetual exercise of the most boisterous passions, the most unremitting despotism on the one part, and degrading submissions on the other. Our children see this, and learn to imitate it; for man is an imitative animal. . . . The parent storms, the child looks on, catches the lineaments of wrath, puts on the same airs in the circle of smaller slaves, gives a loose to his worst of passions, and thus nursed, educated, and daily exercised in tyranny, cannot but be stamped by it with odious peculiarities. The man must be a prodigy who can retain his manners and morals undepraved by such circumstances.

—President of the United States Thomas Jefferson

All honor to Jefferson—to the man who, in the concrete pressure of a struggle for national independence by a single people, had the coolness, forecast and capacity to introduce into a merely revolutionary document, an abstract truth, applicable to all men and all times, and so to embalm it there, that to-day, and in all coming days, it shall be a rebuke and a stumbling-block to the very harbingers of re-appearing tyranny and oppression.

—President of the United States Abraham Lincoln

I had him severely flogged in the presence of his old companions.

—President of the United States Thomas Jefferson

There is no right to resort to violence when you don't get your way.

. . . If you appropriate our sacred symbols for paranoid purposes and compare yourselves to colonial militias who fought for the democracy you now rail against, you are wrong. How dare you suggest that we in the freest nation on Earth live in tyranny! How dare you call yourselves patriots and heroes!

—President of the United States Bill Clinton

The tree of liberty must be refreshed from time to time with the blood of patriots and tyrants. It is it's natural manure.

—President of the United States Thomas Jefferson

This party does not prey on people's prejudices. We appeal to their highest ideals. This is the Party of Lincoln. We believe all people are created equal in the eyes of God and our government.

—United States Speaker of the House Paul Ryan

The separation of infants from their mothers too would produce some scruples of humanity. but this would be straining at a gnat, and swallowing a camel.

—President of the United States Thomas Jefferson

Let Music Swell the Breeze

The sun came back, and a bobwhite whistled behind the hedge. Shadows of sharp rose stems and lolling heads stretched across the doctor's shoes. He plucked a petal, soft as velvet on his manicured fingertips, and thought back to the interview with the radioman. It was the reason he was there in the rose garden—cool, clean fingers rubbing rose petals—waiting on the governor.

A few weeks before, the radioman had asked him onto the show. Generating buzz for the upcoming primaries. Still a few months out, already a dozen names thrown into the ring. They would be important, everyone said. Winner to challenge senate seat, senate seat to determine majority. National audience tuned in, listening for the call to arms. It's the 1770s all over again.

This garden might be 200 years old, he thought, looking at the bodyguard in the black suit and sunglasses leaning against a wrought iron arch. Old plantation architecture. Wide porches with rocking chairs. Corinthian columns propping up porticos.

The 1770s all over again. The video gone viral since. Quick, slick, conservative kids with computers in their pockets, watching, commenting. The radioman—radical—in his booth. Into the mic, onto the air—the mouthpiece of the conservative movement, confirming the doctor as the nation's future. A photo of the doctor—the would-be politician—projected onto a screen beside the booth. Silver-streaked hair, rugged face—wrinkled like a sheet of foil around the eyes—shaved close, scrubbed clean. An American face looking toward the country's future.

Twisting the petal to pulp, he smelled his perfumed fingertips and walked between the flowers. He heard the low hum of someone singing. Then someone answering far away. It sounded familiar, the song, the call and response. And although he couldn't quite catch the tune, he remembered something vague from his childhood. A low-slung, whitewashed church throbbing, his grandfather pulling him away, jerking his hand down the dirt road. He strained to hear, motionless in the garden, but the voices were moving in the other direction.

Before the interview with the radioman—sitting behind his desk at home—he had sung arpeggios to warm up his voice. La-la-la-li-la-la-la. Ma-ma-ma-me-ma-ma-ma. You'll be fine, his wife said, stepping into the room with two bottles of water in her hands. It's a challenge you're ready to meet. Flower-print apron tied around her waist, the pot roast already in the oven. Slow-cooking American Dream. She provided all the support he and the kids would ever need. But remember, she said, placing the bottles on the desk. You're a leader with God in his heart. Not a soldier. Make him know. She turned and whisked herself from the room, pulling closed the French doors behind her.

There was a framed facsimile of the Declaration on the wall behind him. He had memorized it in high school and retained it ever since. The Laws of Nature and Nature's God. Along with the Preamble and the Articles. His ticket to the big leagues. Pictures of Jefferson, Washington, Jackson, Reagan on the walls. All eyes toward the future. The afternoon sunlight slanting through the wooden blinds. Crisp, the grandeur of God.

Warmer still today in the rose garden, and someone singing spirituals far away. He caught the song again, remembered dark faces sweating above purple robes in the little church—the whites of rolling eyes like cartoons he had seen, the dark holes of wailing mouths—swaying in syncopation, doors wide open to the dirt road. His grandfather pulling him away. The memory seemed like some scene from a black and white film, or a postcard of gospel singers. The plantation literature he had read as a child was packed full of black folks' rolling eyeballs. He couldn't remember what was real. Who was that little boy? he wondered.

Smiling, he bowed his head toward the sundial at his feet. In the governor's rose garden, a slant shadow on slabbed stone. Cast from an angle pointing into the past. For the old man is a-waiting for to carry you to freedom. The bobwhite called again behind the hedge. We must save the country from tyranny, he told the radioman. Divine providence, in *our* hands now. Manifest, the destiny. He made him know, all right.

When in the Course

It's the 1770s all over again, he said as the radio show opened. Back to the Constitution's original intent. We're fighting for true individualism. True American conceptualism. Stars and stripes waving behind him. I remember a quote you used on this show, he told the radioman. Something Jefferson wrote to his nephew.

Let me have it, the radioman answered.

He told him to challenge everything. And that's exactly what we're doing. We're living in a less free America, the doctor said. We're fighting for liberty—for the foundational core beliefs upon which this country was founded—and I'm not sitting silent in the saddle anymore.

The radioman clapped. Hot dog, he answered. Then welcome to the fight, my friend.

There are two questions of supreme importance, the doctor continued. The first: Who's sovereign? He held up his index finger—alone in his office at home—imagining himself talking into a camera. The second, he said: What's the role of government? He held up his middle finger, paused. His wife nodded at him from behind the French doors. And Thomas Jefferson, he said, answered both of those questions in the second paragraph of the Declaration. He said that God is sovereign, that we are created in his image, and that we're therefore guaranteed life—from the moment of conception, let's be clear about that—life, liberty, and the pursuit of happiness. And that government only exists to secure these rights. That government derives its power from the people—not the other way around.

The radioman clapped again. You're speaking my language, he said. Really hittin' the nail on the head.

The hammer—his wife had called him when it was all over. Did you hear him? He called you the hammer.

Now, in the garden, he took his coat off and stepped into the grass—dew-laden, sweet-smelling—away from the mansion on the hill. Just holler when he's ready, he said over his shoulder. Playing cool, as if he didn't know why he was there. The man in the black suit nodded. Black sunglasses, stone-faced, plugged in through his ear. The whole world listening. The sundial ticking.

You're speaking my language, the radioman had said. But I speak Jefferson. I'm fluent in the founding fathers. What about these twenty-somethings who don't care two bits about our nation's history. What are you going to do about them?

They do care, the doctor answered, they do. But the country—and young people especially—are drifting away from traditional parties. Perhaps it's time for a third. One that represents those true Americans out there who realize we need revolution. Not reform.

Hot dog, the radioman laughed. Folks, I think we have a real contender.

The hammer, his wife said.

Yes sir, the doctor answered. I find myself thinking back to something Ronald Reagan said when he left the Democratic party.

What's that? the radioman asked.

I didn't leave them, the doctor said, pounding his fist on the desk. They left me.

The listeners ate it up. Fuzzy past with old granddad, country on the up and up then. A shining city on a hill. Still a dozen to beat before the big fight. But he was on his way. The crates of tea jettisoned, the harbor tinged with the blood to come.

Pick-a-nick Patterns

He wandered down the slope, beneath the occasional shade of twisted live oaks and sprawling magnolias, past redbuds and tupelos and dogwood trees, his hands clasped behind his back, the sun on his face. Two black women in red gingham dresses walked past him in the opposite direction. One wore a turban on her head, and on top of the turban, a reed-woven basket, enormous and bleached white by the sun. He stopped and watched them—fluid bodies beneath thin fabric. Cut from the same cloth, costumed stereotypes ambling barefoot over the grounds. The pale soles of their feet in languid unison over the red brick. Up toward the big house, doing what?

Were those the singers he had heard? There'd be trouble for the governor if anyone saw those two. The liberal media would have a field day. The radioman would rebut them. And if he himself was senator, would he have to weigh in? The radioman had been called a hothead—and worse—but so had Paul Revere. You don't rally troops with a calm voice. You do it with fire in your throat.

I can't think of a single thing working against you, the radioman had said. I don't understand why you're not running away with this thing.

I'm not hiding, the doctor had told him. I mean what I say, and I'm willing to back it up. Numbers on the tip of his tongue. He was doing better with women, minorities, and college kids than one would think. His opponents out of touch with the constituents they wished to represent. We the people. Revolution not reform. No apologies—never—only truth and action.

The flowerbeds that flanked the bench on which he sat reminded him of his wife's apron. Bright. Smiling at him from behind the French doors. Someone's job to take care of these flowers, he thought. Good honest work! Those women in red gingham? Why were they dressed like that? Barefoot! The press would have a field day.

His eyes drifted over the grass to the long hedge that walled in the yard, smoke rising from the pine trees behind them. A lot of forest back there, even in the heart of the city. The frail plumes of smoke looked like the cookfires of another time.

He stretched his legs in front of him and imagined soldiers supping in lulls of fighting. Far from home, scribbling love letters to wives, sending rag dolls to children. Thinking about death and freedom. Someone with a fiddle as the sun set. Men fighting a losing war, a lost cause. And yet they soldiered on against encroachment. Shadow men whispering of lives left behind. Revolution, revolution, not reform.

He thought of his own wife and children—front and center—in his run for office. The image mattered. He had learned as much at the guru's institute all those years ago. He had trained for politics before he became a doctor, and now he had come full circle. The hammer, his wife said when the interview was over. Tap-tap-tapping away.

Duty, to Throw Off

When he introduced the doctor—the would-be senator—the radioman made note of the man's numerous children. You're an OBGYN, he said, and you have seven kids, so I'm assuming you know what's causing that.

The doctor chuckled. I think I have an idea, he answered.

So why, asked the radioman, why in the world would you want to get involved in politics?

It's not political, the doctor answered. It's the act of a serving citizen. When duty calls, you must answer, he said. Our generation is going to pass on a less free America unless we stand up. And I'm not going to look into my child's face, into the faces of the nine-thousand children I've delivered, and shrug my shoulders when they ask—fifteen years from now—where were you in the fight for liberty?

He imagined them on the grass below him. An army of children he had delivered. Sitting in front of their pitched pup tents and campfires, looking up to their leader. Now galloping through camp on a white horse, his saber in the air. Their question—not, where were you?—but, how can we carry on?

I was raised by a single mother, he told the radioman. She liked to talk about this country as a land of opportunity. The opportunity to get up every time you fall down. That's the individual's right. And America is the only place in the world where the individual trumps the collective. Our Constitution, based on Judeo-Christian tenets, protects the individual—from the moment of his conception, until his dying breath—from the government.

Big government, the radioman chimed in. Progressivism, what they call it. He laughed. Before the progressive era, he said, we didn't have the problems we have today.

That's right, the doctor answered.

Welfare state, people hopping the borders. They wouldn't come if there wasn't free stuff.

No sir.

Don't get me wrong, the radioman continued. I'm *for* immigration. *Legal* immigration.

Provided by the Constitution, the doctor answered.

That's what this country's founded on—competition. I *want* people competing for my job. I want that. Let the best man win, I say.

The doctor stood up from the bench and continued down the slope toward the hedge, wondering if the governor would endorse him. Strings of smoke slithered from the treetops. He heard running water from the forest. Watched as more black women in red gingham disappeared into the cut hedges below him. Too far away to tell if they were the same ones he had seen before. Now more of them—five, six—apparitions glancing back at him. Then gone into the green.

Down the slope and over a brick path that ran along the square-cut hedge. Evergreen, ten feet tall, used to make mazes, he thought. Need a ball of string to get out like the Greek hero did. His future was a labyrinth, unknowable.

With Freedom's Holy Light

You say you've seen my show, the radioman said. So, you must know what I'm going to ask you next.

Oh yes, the doctor answered. You're going to ask me about my soul.

And how is it?

I'll tell you, the doctor answered. I'm here today because I was born again. This is a spiritual battle we're fighting. Romans twelve, verse nine says to hate evil and cling to good. Everyone knows that. But the first part of that verse is even more important. It calls for genuine love. And that's how we're going to change hearts and minds. I can hit the nail on the head all day, he said, but we're not going to change hearts with a hammer. This is what we do. We go to the people—the people who disagree with us—with loving and kindness, we go to them and discuss these things. As Americans.

He launched into dual federalism, tap-tap, ambassador of the sovereign state. As if there was no seventeenth amendment, he said. Tap-tap. You must understand that contract. If you can't, you cannot lead.

Quotes from the Constitution. Quotes from the Bible. Revolution. Tap-tapping away.

Wow, said the radioman. I've talked to a lot of politicians, and it usually takes me a while to warm up. But you, sir, he said. You are so well read, and you've taken the time to think out your platform. I believe you're the best damn candidate I've ever talked to. And I mean it!

Thank you, the doctor answered. I'm so honored. I just believe that liberty is so simple. We're on the cusp of something big here. Our grandchildren are either going to look back and thank us or else they're going to ridicule us. And I want to be standing on the front lines with you. I want to be fighting the good fight.

Dark.

A deep green darkness on the other side of the hedge. He pulled his head back into the sunlight. What an effect. Following the brick pathway, he looked for the place where the women had passed through. Black skin, red gingham, the sound of running water. No one at all on the timeless green slope above him. Serene.

Where was the bodyguard in the black suit? Was there still time to investigate before his meeting with the governor? Just a peek, he told himself. How far back did the grounds go, anyway? Wild back there. In the middle of the capital city. Strange. People from another time wandering through the landscape.

Wind rushed through the isolated hillside trees, shaking their limbs. The doctor felt small. Like a child crouched against the hedge, staring over his shoulder at the sky. Everything as bright as a Disney cartoon. These were the winds of change. Seven crows alighted from an oak tree on the hill. He counted them. Cawing. Talking together in black-beak code. He remembered sitting in front of a console television in his parents' living room. Rolling eyeballs. Jazz birds dancing in hiccup steps. Jive talking. Fat cigars smoking in their clapping beaks. His grandfather smoking cigarettes.

Black kites against the blue sky, their shadows sliding over the ground. Constellations bleeding into each other. As if chained together, into the woodland beyond.

Light and Transient Causes

A break in the hedge farther down. Not a doorway, but a place where people might slip through. Big women, those black ladies, he thought. He looked up the sunny slope again. He no longer heard running water. Or, rather, the sound had changed to something else. The susurration of singing. Bodies sweating in a church. Murmur from the ground up. The wind dying as he ducked into the prickling.

Sharp fingers scraping against him, nails biting his flesh, pulling his shirt. He squeezed into the dark.

Ten degrees cooler in the shade, winter clutching to the shadows back here. Gash of light piercing the hedge where he stepped through. It would be easy to find his way back, he thought. The point where the gardener gave up. A wall between groomed nature and the real thing. Virgin forests, the early explorers had said.

Pine needles underfoot, he let his eyes adjust to the absence of light. The trees bigger than they should have been. Thick trunks standing straight and tall. Wild and empty beneath them. Sentinels for hundreds of years. He put his jacket back on, took tentative steps into the seeming forest, wondering how it could be. Orange fires glowing on the ground in the distance, carcasses spinning on spits. He had seen smoke rising from the treetops, hadn't he? Antic shapes danced before the flames, throwing shadows long and slant. He remembered the whitewashed church again, the bright bodies roiling inside. Purple. What tricks back here in the dark?

There were voices like water all around him. Rushing. Crows cawing in the treetops and someone screaming. A woman in labor, he thought. On the forest floor? It couldn't be. Nighttime back here, a green nightmare. The screaming stopped, and he wondered if he had imagined it. He lost his balance and couldn't catch it again. Saw dark shapes hurrying to and fro.

Fear welled up inside of him and he stopped cold. Leaned against a tree trunk to steady himself. Taking deep breaths, he tried to calm down by recounting his steps. What is this? he said out loud, looking at the sunlight streaming through the hedge. A different day on the other side. Sunny springtime, falling bright. Smooth lawn, the smell of cut grass, men in black suits with sunglasses, plugged in through their ears. Calm down, doctor, he told himself, trying to smile. You're at the governor's mansion. Here by his request. You're about to be endorsed.

He turned again—away from the light—peered into the gloom of the woods. It was no mistake. There were fires burning and dark shapes dancing spindly through the low glow. A deep murmur from nowhere and everywhere welling up in his ears, a gathering. Someone yelled and someone answered. Preparations for something. An event at the mansion?

Hadn't he seen stacks of tables and chairs as he entered the gardens? Surely, they held functions on the governor's lawn. Pig-pickin fundraisers in the style of the Old South. Black waiters and waitresses to complete the scene? A bit old-fashioned, he thought. Dressed in red gingham? Barefoot? Cookfires secreted in the deep wood? He imagined dark men in black tuxedos, toting silver platters. If someone caught wind, he thought again, the press would have a field day.

Pastel-Painted Past

We've made mistakes, he told the radioman. In regard to skin color and gender. We've had the hard conversations that needed having, and we've fixed what needed fixing.

Animal shapes. Animal sounds. Plotting back here in the dark. Perhaps he should say something to the governor. Perhaps he should head back—

Someone screamed again, and he began walking toward the fires in the distance, determined to figure out what was going on. His shoes sibilant in the pine needles. Unmistakable, that noise. A woman fully dilated and pushing. Hadn't he heard it nine-thousand times?

There are more conversations to be had, he said during the interview. The fight for life today is the same one we've fought before. During the Civil Rights era. During the suffrage movement. If a country can't protect the most innocent of innocents, how can it accomplish anything? He shrugged his shoulders in his office at home. Shook his head while staring at framed photos of his children. I'm talking from the heart here, he told the radioman. We must protect the rights of the individual against those of the collective. That's who we are.

Orange shine leaping on black skin. There. Then gone. Closer, between the trees, shining eyes. Blinking out of existence. Singers in a church, heads back, throats exposed. He stopped and listened for the woman in labor, his mouth open to call out, to offer help, but something snagged his elbow.

Someone's hand. Holding tight as he tried to wrench free.

Let go! he screamed, surprised at his own voice.

But the hand pinched harder, a noose around his arm. Whirling him like a rag doll—until he faced the opposite direction.

Let go! he screamed again, adrenaline pumping through his veins. He threw his hands up to protect his face, his muscles tight, an animal on its haunches.

He opened his eyes. The man who had grabbed him held his hands up as if to show he meant no harm. A white man with white hair on his head, wearing a green suit and a green cravat, pale stockings on his legs, leather shoes with golden buckles.

Behind him, a group of white people with powdered faces in the getup of some bygone era. Victorian? Pre-Victorian? He was no fashion buff. Bizarre. All eyes on him. Puffed pastels, gold embroidering, layers and layers of lace. A cache of Easter eggs spilled among the tree roots. The man in the white wig was smiling. No need to be frightened, sir, he said, raising his eyebrows. 'Tis but an animal passing her litter.

The women behind him giggled into their white-gloved hands.

What? the doctor asked.

We must keep the group together, the man continued. All of us. He half turned, speaking to the rest of them. The surprises of the evening, he said, will not be half as delightful if you peek behind the curtains like a sneak.

The ladies giggled again.

Come. He winked, holding out his hand. We mustn't keep Jefferson waiting.

The doctor stared at him. Jefferson? he asked.

Yes, nodded the other. Don't you know where you are? He laughed. The others behind him as well, taking their cue from him. Come, he said—waving them forward—or else we'll be late.

His long coat tails whipped behind him as he turned and continued up the path between the trees. Pale figures, two by two, behind the bright-suited man. Through the woods, the doctor lagging. Looking behind him for the gap in the hedge, which he could no longer make out.

What of the women in gingham? Barefoot through the woods. The one screaming in the dark? Where was she?

He remembered the open mouths of those singers in the whitewashed church. Remembered babies spilling from between their mothers' legs as if they had traveled some immeasurable distance. Into this world from another.

Was this some sort of reenactment? he wondered. The costumes were over the top. He stumbled up the path behind them, his feet sinking into the ground, until a woman caught his arm and buoyed him along.

Among the Powers of Earth

Easily impressed, are you? she asked.

He stared at her face. Powdered skin, pink cheeks, red lips. Her body pulled tight at the waist—corseted—the dress billowing below, hiding her lower half. What type of game is this? he asked.

She laughed. Just you wait, she said. Have you never been before?

He turned away. Tried to see through the woods to the low burning fires. Something slick and fat twisting slowly on a spit. Tried to see back to the shadows dancing. But the woman pulled him along. He thought he could hear a deep moan from the forest floor. But it was farther away now. The sound of a thousand years—of time's beginning—down there. He couldn't see anything as they continued upward. Tree-tunneled, everything closing in.

Been where? he asked.

She turned toward him. Here, she said, to Monticello.

He laughed. Monticello? he asked. There were stone steps cut into the walkway now. He picked up a nail on the ground. Come along, the woman said.

Who made these nails? he wondered. Who cut these steps? Who swept the wooded walk? He heard a snatch of song. Who watered the flowers in the flowerpots? Who trimmed the long hedge? Who tended the fire? Monticello? he whispered again.

But the woman didn't answer.

Long arms of white mist stretched between the trees. Upward, like monks to an altar. Shrouded. Disappearing.

Up toward heaven. Then solid again, struggling up the grade in felt shoes—wooden-bottomed—calves bulging through stockings. Manly men dressed effeminately. Black strings swinging at the bottoms of white braids. The women ridiculous in their dresses, stumbling along, clinging tightly to their pastel beaus. Faux elegance in dress-up clothes. Teetering beneath the thinning canopy. Fragile. Magnificent, said the woman holding onto his arm. A veil of smoke snaked between them. Her eyes shining, then fading, then gone.

What is this? the doctor asked as she dissolved before his eyes. The gloved hand vanishing. His perfumed fingers empty but for the nail he had found on the ground. The rest of them gone as well.

There was certainly no hill this big on the property. Feet scurried through the woods around him—unseen—different from the clip-clop of the actors. Furtive, quick feet over damp leaves. Barefoot. Invisible shapes toiling, eyeballs rolling through the mist. Glimpses, then blinking to nothing. He called out to them. Asked them for help. But there was never an answer. Only shadows.

From Every Mountain Side

Onward and upward. No chance of descending into the green gloom now. The 1770s all over again. Apparitions of a rolling landscape through the mist below. The moon silver up above him, a nickel shining in the sky. And the dipper pouring starlight onto the ground. But it had been morning in the rose garden, hadn't it? Bright the pathway before him, crisp the air, the mist receding as if by command.

He heard someone whisper behind him and turned to watch. Quick from one side of the path to the other, a group of black boys in rags. One lagging behind, dragging a doll through the dirt, looking up at him for an instant, then gone. Grabbed by a long, dark arm and swallowed by the rhododendron. Afraid. The doctor called out. Stepped toward them. Stopped short when he heard them scurrying away. Then turned and kept on, the ground leveling beneath him.

The path widening. People talking up ahead, laughing. The shining rustle of glass on glass. Everything opening. The strong smell of mint and mustard seed. He saw the woman again. And the rest of them, beneath wrought iron chandeliers hanging from tree branches. Soft, the glow of candles. This was the guests' retreat. The doings down below out of sight, out of mind. Something greasy on the spit, dripping. The last fingers of mist snatched away by some unseen force. To reveal the mansion on the hilltop, the veil torn from his eyes. Impossible, he thought. He couldn't think.

Monticello brightly lit. Nickeled moonlight from the sky. For the old man is a-waiting for to carry you to freedom. Soft strands of violin strings singing melodies into the swift nighttime. People bowing, ladies laughing, a party. Silver brilliance flipped into the past. An apparition, richly clad. Real, unreal, real. Shining beacon to the world below. White on white on white. How could it be?

She waved to him, the woman, an amber glass of liquid pinched in her fingertips. Come, she motioned, come. Beneath a canvas tent-top, black men poured drinks from glass pitchers. Black waiters with silver platters walked between the white folks. It can't be, he thought. Tiny below the big house, everyone. The architecture of the New World, built by the New World's architect.

Furtive figures quiet-trotting between the house and trees. Working with averted eyes. Shadows of themselves.

Blood pulsing hot. Antic shapes come tumbling from his head, dancing Africa into the lowlands. Down below this ethereal castle in the clouds. Slaves. Breathe. But his breath was hard to catch. Running from him now. Temple of a Grecian god. Lightheaded, he swayed back and forth, put a hand out to catch himself. It couldn't be. Speak in tongues before this night's over. Possessed. Progress. Freedom prophet, scripture speaker. Here on this nickel-plated platform, a vision. The Acropolis of a nation. Come to dine with President Jefferson, thank you very much. Revolution ringing from the land. Revolution not reform. He heard his voice echoing from the interview. It's the 1770s all over again.

Then the sound of bare feet hustling through the woods. Ring. White light framing the vision before him. Ring. Everything fuzzy, the woman with her glass up-tilted. Ring. Waving. Come, ring, come. His knees upon the ground, here to praise this holy land. Hives of activity all around, unseen. Ring, hustle, ring, bustle, bound, ring. Blood on his hands, chained to freedom's champion, ring. Bound up in this place. A halo-headed man stepping proudly through the party's guests. Unalienable rights, he was shouting. Property, property, property. Ring. Square-shouldered. But when a long train of abuses. Straight as a gun barrel. Ring. The savior of a nation, revolution on his lips. Absolute Despotism, he shouted. Patient sufferance. Absolute Tyranny. Ring. Blood on his hands. Ring. A history of repeated injuries and usurpations, he shouted. Everyone raised their glasses in the air and cheered. He saw nine-thousand babies on the forest floor. Ring. Throwing long shadows through the trees.

Jefferson come to baptize them with sticky fingers. Ring. Come to baptize them with perfumed hands. Ring. Come to baptize them where their fathers died. Ring.

Sweet land of the pilgrims' pride. Ring. A woman screaming down there. The doctor could not breathe, his mind speared on a spit and sweating above the flames. Upon his knees on the packed earth. In penitence. A woman writhing on the ground. Jefferson approached, and the doctor noticed the buttons on his leather shoes were gold. Ring. Down below, the sound up-swelling. Ring, ring. Crackling through the phone line. Ring, America, ring. Phoned-in from the beginning. Hammering away. Ring. He heard her splayed upon the forest floor—alone. No one to guide her toward the light—ring—on the mountain top. Where one white man reached down to another. Ring. Trembling through time.

And for the support of this Declaration, Jefferson said, his hand upon the doctor's head. With a firm reliance on the protection of divine Providence. The doctor mouthed the words. Sobbing. We mutually pledge to each other our Lives, our Fortunes and our sacred Honor. Ring. The guests erupted in applause. Ring. The doctor cut his hands on the nail and wept.

Down below, a woman wailed in the wilderness, her voice ringing off the stars and stripes of the firmament. Splayed among the rocks and rills. Ring. Alone beneath the templed hills—ring—wishing her birthed child unborn. For the old man is a-waiting. Let freedom ring. Ring. Let freedom ring. Ring. Let freedom ring.

Tricky Dick

1.

Pregnancy doesn't just happen by itself.

I know, he answered over his shoulder. They shuffled up the brick walkway with the long plastic folding table between them. Small and clumsy beneath the fat-columned university buildings, the table cumbersome, the world asleep.

He held the front end and led the way, though it was she who knew where they were going. President of the Students for Life Coalition. She also carried two trifold cardboard posters plastered with colored photographs of dismembered fetuses and bullet-point statistics about the history of abortion-based genocide. Everything square and awkward as they shuffled along in little jerks, their voices enormous in the silence.

Personal responsibility, she said, trying to get a better grip on the table. Half the country doesn't know what it is. She stumbled and shook her blonde hair from her face, convinced it was catching on the pimple that had appeared that morning on the tip of her nose.

He stopped and offered to carry the posters again.

No, she said. I told you how they were stolen last year. The table rested on the ground between them. I could only blame myself if it happened again. That's exactly what

I'm talking about. Personal responsibility. He was staring at the pimple. She could tell. I'm the president now, and we have work to do.

They continued up the brick walkway—one behind the other—to the quad in admonished silence. The university was a ghost town this morning. The grass clipped, the walkways spotless, the confederate soldiers confident on their marble pedestals, their bronzed eyes pointed toward the north. It was during these days of early autumn—when the halls filled up with college kids and the leaves turned orange and jingled like paper coins on their branches—that hearts and minds could be changed. Go out there tap-tap-tapping like a hammer, said the doctor politician on the radio. Tell the truth and shame the devil, the good reverend always said.

So, you've heard about the Muslims at the chapel, right? The boy looked back to check on her again. Cheerleader-like, petite, blonde-headed, blue-eyed, the girl next door, the president. He tried not to look at the pimple on her nose, tried not to look at her thighs where her shorts had ridden up.

Go on, she said, pushing the table forward. We're going up past the poplar tree. And no, I haven't heard anything about the chapel.

He walked faster. The call to prayer, he said. You haven't heard? He paused, but she didn't answer. The campus Muslims, he continued. They're doing a call to prayer from the steeple on Fridays.

No, she said, dropping her end of the table.

They got a PA system and everything. It's supposed to start in a few weeks.

At the campus chapel? she asked, pulling her shorts down in two quick jerks.

He nodded, and she looked past him to the copper dome of the library. Her forehead and eyes crinkling up as the sun peeked over the roof.

He squinted back at her. The pimple was bigger than it had been an hour ago when he met her at the union in the dark. A few small ones had freckled her chin when they went on their first and only date last year, caked in the wrong shade of makeup. He had wanted to wipe her face clean.

I don't believe it, she said.

He concentrated on her mouth. Do I look like I'm kidding? he asked.

OK. Then what's being done about it?

He shrugged. Nothing, I don't think. I asked the College Conservative Chair, but he didn't seem to know about it either.

The chair? she asked. I'm the president.

I know, but you're already so busy, he answered, with all this Students for Life stuff.

I haven't even heard about it.

It was in the student paper.

Liberal media, she muttered, watching the sun inch over the green patina dome. When she shook her head, the pimple wobbled on her nose.

What are you looking at? she asked, turning to the boy. Come on. We have work to do.

2.

You decide what you want.
You work for it.
You do not bargain.
You do not flinch.

Downstairs, she had demanded an air conditioning unit from the Community Director. The same unit, she insisted, that had been in her room the year before, but which had—mysteriously—disappeared over the summer. Take, take, take, she said, shaking her head. Is that how public universities work? The Community Director said she didn't know what she was talking about.

They were reading my blog, the president answered, her hands on her hips. They contacted me about my editorial in the school paper before the summer started. Infringing on my right to free speech. Again, the Community Director promised that if the room was slated as an air-conditioned single, then she would get a unit as soon as one was made available.

Made available. Bureaucratic baloney. The president walked up the outdoor stairwell toward her room, wondering if she should post something to social media. They wanted to make her miserable, since they couldn't shut her up. Shadowy members of the liberal elite. Orwellian. The doctor politician said they needed revolution not reform.

She had tacked up a couple of old campaign posters and an American flag in her dorm room, but it would never feel like home. She was a spy in the belly of the beast. A voice in the wilderness, the good reverend said. Sighing, she sat down at the desk beside the window where the A/C unit should have been. Her lips fluttered as she read what she had already written on the screen.

> *I'm a lively young lady who has a lot to say. I like my politics red, my fences white, and my skies blue. I'm a Future First Lady who grew up watching and listening to the Radioman on my daddy's knee. The promise ring he gave me still hugs my finger. It's a reminder of his*

love for me and of the everlasting love of Jesus Christ our Lord and Savior. We are one nation under God.

Go with your gut, the guru had said when she attended his famous summer institute. Don't apologize for speaking your mind.

I feel it is my job to step into that uncomfortable zone and say what needs to be said. The whole country is walking on eggshells now, and I'm not going to take it anymore. I'm offended by those who are offended, and you should be too. Sitting on my daddy's knee, listening to the Radioman, I developed a keen interest for politics and current events, an interest that has fueled my growth from the youngster I was into the woman I am: the Founder and President of the Future First Ladies, President of the Students for Life Coalition, and President of the Southeast Branch of the College Conservatives. My grandmother was queen of the Azalea Belles, as was my mother, as was I. But today there's a war being waged on heritage. We are witnessing it happen before our very eyes. There are those that want us to forget who we are and where we come from. But I will not forget. And neither should you. This is the 1770s all over again, as the good doctor says, and I know which side I'm fighting for. Do you?

She sat back in her chair and stared at the computer screen, the digitized border of red, white, and blue, the text in a font imitating calligraphy over a scroll of yellow parchment paper: her Declaration of Independence. The scroll seemed a bit too much. But the good reverend always said doubt was the tool of the devil. If you're right, be righteous. Glory be.

Yawning, she stood and stared at herself in the mirror hanging on the closet door. Her nose looked like it was drooping. Like the whole thing had gotten longer, the red tip bulbous and dangling. It didn't hurt when she touched it, though, like pimples usually do. Instead, she felt pins and needles in the backs of her knees. She shivered even though her room was a sauna.

Not ready, she said out loud, sounding like her mother. High school acne days. Warm washcloths on her forehead. Don't mess, her mother said. Smothering her in the pink room. You'll be a parent yourself one day, the guru had told her when she complained about the prudish clothes her mother made her pack to the summer institute. The good book says honor thy father and mother. He looked her up and down. You still look mighty fine to me, he said. Pins and needles.

The mission, she typed, *is to acquaint, familiarize, support, and produce a sense of pride in what it means to be a modern yet traditional conservative woman. We are the Future First Ladies of this country.* At the bottom of the mission statement, she typed in all caps *FUTURE FIRST LADIES HONOR: GOD, FAMILY, COUNTRY*, then flipped the laptop closed. Satisfied.

As she rolled into bed sweating, a warm washcloth on her face, she wondered about the A/C unit and whether she was doing too much. She was the only one on campus who had been to the guru's training and was trying to lead by example. The A/C unit didn't really matter. It was the principle of the thing. How it looked to the world. The image! The image! The image! the guru liked to shout.

She thought about the boy staring at her nose that morning, and touched it again, a shiver running up her legs. She found her hand between her thighs. Don't mess, she whispered to herself.

3.

The doorbell echoed from the vaulted ceiling like glass blowing in the wind. Her key didn't work. This was twice in three years that her parents had changed the locks. There must have been talk of intruders again. Riots in cities across the country. She recalled the black kids who had snuck into the community pool the summer before she left. The incident that followed was unfortunate, but what did they expect? The neighborhood watch was on high alert afterward. Men with guns patrolled the streets.

That's some pimple, her mother said when she opened the door.

It's good to see you too, mother. The president brushed by her.

I didn't mean it like that, her mother said, watching the pink quilted duffle bag bounce up the carpeted steps. She couldn't think of anything else to say. Supper's at six, she finally managed, as the president turned toward her bedroom. Come down and talk to me before your father gets home, she added. I want to hear how your week went, honey. Afterward, she wandered the living room looking at framed family photos on the walls.

During supper, the president's mother tried to joke. Once again, she said to her husband, our little president has failed to bring home a first man.

The room smelled of canned biscuits and rotisserie chicken. Rice, gravy, and green beans steamed in glass bowls on the tabletop.

Come on, mom, the president said. She made a little circle in the rice with her fork. I'm already stressed out—which is probably the reason for this. She pointed at her nose, gravy dripping from the prongs.

Honey, her mother said, don't use your fork like that. It's unladylike.

The president didn't seem to hear. Am I the only one who cares? she asked. She dropped her fork onto her plate and mumbled something about personal responsibility.

Well, honey, her mother said, you might get more work done if you didn't come home every weekend.

The president was incredulous. You don't want me visiting?

She didn't mean that, her dad said quickly. He shook his head at his wife. Of course we want you coming home, baby. Every chance you get.

He reached his hand across the linen tablecloth and took her hand in his. They wore matching promise rings, a sapphire in hers for the virgin mother. He had vowed to protect her at the fancy Italian restaurant just after she turned sixteen. There had been candles flickering and a man with black hair and a mustache playing sad songs on a violin. The instrument had sounded like a woman's voice as they rolled spaghetti on their spoons. She would be pure, she had promised. That was her half of the deal. She had said she loved him, and they had laughed about the dark hair on the arms of the Italian violinist. Her father's hands were darker now from playing so much golf. You're my princess, he had said that night, and you deserve the best. He gave her the pink-plated pistol at the daddy-daughter prom later that night, and she would never forget opening the hard plastic case as if it contained a corsage. They went to the range the next day and shot at paper targets of bad guys. She still remembered crying when he put the ring on her finger. You'll never know how much you mean to me, he had said as the waiter brought tiramisu.

We want you coming home every chance you get, he said again, his eyes going soft.

She looked up at him and smiled, wiped her eyes with her napkin. I'm sorry, she said, I'm just stressed out.

Picking up her utensils, she turned to her mom and tried to joke. What boy wants to look at this thing anyway? she said, pointing with her fork.

Her mom smiled and said she didn't care about the boys. Only that her daughter was happy. And that utensils be used the way they were intended.

4.

She had gone viral before. Back when she was campaigning for the doctor politician and caught a university professor calling her a spoiled brat on camera. You're a good-hearted simpleton, the professor said, not paying attention to the phone in her hand. Too dumb not to be duped. She captured it all on video.

It's the 1770s all over again, she shot back, a head shorter than the professor. We want revolution not reform. Your students are the ones being brainwashed.

The professor called her privilege-all-dressed-up-as-a-sorority-girl. Angry, liberal, elite, talking down his nose to a young woman with a differing opinion. Who was sexist, after all? A million views. People knew who she was after that. Eventually, the professor lost his job.

This time she threatened to sue when the woman grabbed the poster from the table. Safe spaces and trigger warnings be damned, hers was a generation of pussies. Women like you are sad, the president said. You act with your lady parts not your lady smarts. This was a tagline for the Future First Ladies that she had been wanting to test. Already, this video was bigger than the first. Trending on both sides of the aisle.

Afterward, somebody spray-painted her dorm room door: *You should have been aborted bitch.* Typical, she told the student paper, standing beside the door. Typical, the nightly news. She wouldn't let them remove the paint. Typical, she told the radioman when he asked her onto the show. When your opponents are adolescent vandals, it's not so hard to be the bigger man.

Her mom called, hysterical, demanding she come home. But the president sent pictures of police officers in the lobby and explained how the wall of blue supported her. Her father offered to drive down and stay with her, and when she refused, he made sure that she still had protection. She sent him a photo of her doing a Charlie's Angels pose in her dorm room with her pink-plated pistol.

The video clip was only a few minutes long, but brevity made for high viewership. It was a graduate student who grabbed the poster. Maybe an adjunct professor. Overweight and frumpy in a khaki getup and thick leather shoes, glasses and mousy brown hair. They had been arguing before the tape started, a few students loafing in the grass around them, whispering about the photos of bloody fetuses and babies' body parts. The president said something about murder, and that's when the grad student—red-faced—pounded her fists on the plastic table. The president had whispered for the puppy dog boy to take a video. They had hoped for something like this. It opened with the angry woman playing tug-of-war with the president.

And I don't have to be ashamed, she was shouting about her own abortion.

Yes, you do, the president shouted back. I'm sorry for your loss, and you should be too. Earnest in her short-shorts, not missing a beat. Control the image, the guru always said. She only wished that pimple hadn't been in the video.

It's not that bad, her mother said on the phone. You know, it almost looks like—well. She giggled. You're beautiful anyway, she said. You kept your composure, unlike that ugly girl. And now this interview with the radioman! Good gracious. You're a celebrity.

She felt bad for that woman, she told the radioman. She really did. What a terrible weight to carry! He replayed the part of the video where she told the graduate student that God would forgive her if she only asked.

The woman's eyes bulged, and her face filled up with blood. Bitch, she yelled at the president. You and your god can stay the fuck out of my pants! They had to bleep it on TV.

Who would want to get in those pants anyway? the president joked with the Students for Life Coalition. They all laughed. Below the student union, in the burgundy room with the beige carpet and the black plastic chairs. This is the perfect visual, she explained from her podium, the YouTube video pulled up on the projector screen—paused in the middle of the action. Can you see how much smaller I am? That's partly the camera angle. She winked at the puppy dog boy. I'm pitted against this bloated giant. You see? It's perfect because we're an army of Davids. This was a line she had used with the radioman. An army of Davids fighting for the rights of the unborn. And every time we face a Goliath—she pointed to the screen—we will strike her down!

They all clapped.

The perfect visual except for that pimple, she thought. In the comments below the video, the liberal trolls called her Pinocchio.

You must stand tall, she told the coalition. You're doing the Lord's work. Expect to be persecuted. Of course, not everyone saw the video the same way. People spitting down the dormitory stairwell at her, hate in the eyes of her fellow students. It was part and parcel, she told the coalition. Being persecuted meant they were doing something right.

Even in front of her friends, though, she kept thinking about the pimple.

5.

She started wearing scarves and turtlenecks to class though it wasn't yet close to cold enough. She kept her hands in front of her face, teased her hair wild, kept her head down. She stopped challenging the liberal drivel of her professors. In the back of the classroom, she re-watched the video streaming across news feeds, fueled by subsequent interviews. She was tired.

We need you back on the quad, the boy said in her bedroom. It's a circus down there, and people want to see you. They think you're scared.

That's ridiculous, she said, her voice sounding muddled. I'm working on this call to prayer thing. I can't do everything, you know.

She had met him at the door with the pistol in her hand and was now sitting at her desk, holding her face in her hands.

You're the strongest girl I know, he said. But the spray-painted door—that's scary.

I'm not scared, she said again.

I know, he answered. Who else would have the balls to keep a gun in their dorm room? It's just that—

Don't tell anyone about that, she interrupted, her voice small and far away.

He put his hand on her shoulder, and she flinched. If it's about this—he pulled his hand away—this pimple or whatever—

It's not, she said.

All those trolls commenting on the video—

That's not it, she said, shaking her head. I'm just working on this call to prayer thing. It almost sounded like she was crying.

I disabled the comments on the video, he said. I'm here if you ever need anything. He paused. I can even stay over if you want.

She tightened her grip on the gun, and he stepped back toward the door. These fucking assholes are going to pay, he said.

6.

You're too stressed, honey. Her mother held open the front door. It must be this media coverage. She raised her eyebrows at the scarf wrapped around her daughter's face. I can't believe you stayed in your room after they spray-painted it.

The president brushed past her. Are you sure you're safe? her mother asked. We put a new alarm system in last week. The president plodded up the stairs, her bag bouncing behind her. People have been calling about that video, her mother said. I can't even watch it.

While her mother fussed in the kitchen, the president and her father watched recorded episodes of the radioman on TV. A prophet swinging the sword of God. Her dad sat in the leather recliner, rubbing Mary Todd's belly.

You look like Granddaddy, the president said, smiling at her dad.

Her father kept his eyes fixed on the TV. I hope I'm not that old yet, he said.

You remember, though? she asked. Watching the radioman with him?

He turned his head, still scratching Mary's belly, and asked if she thought about Granddaddy a lot.

Of course, she said. I'm starting that new organization, you know—the Future First Ladies—and I'm writing about him. About you too, she said.

Her dad raised his eyebrows. About me? he asked.

Well—about how I got interested in politics. Watching the radioman with y'all and listening to Grandaddy talk. She smiled and cleared her voice. I had eight brothers and sisters, she imitated. We were dirt-poor country folk.

Her dad chimed in. And if I can make something of myself, then anyone can!

She laughed—Amen—but as her shoulders shook, she felt her nose flapping against her lips. Her father turned back toward the TV, squeezing the poodle in his hands.

The president sighed. He would have pointed out this pimple too, she said after a minute. Remember how he made me wash my face with egg yolks?

Her father smiled. He used to tell your aunts how fat they'd gotten when they came home from college. He looked at his daughter. At least they're feeding you up there, he would say.

She feigned surprise.

Not you, he said, laughing. He looked her up and down. You still look pretty good to me. On the TV, the radioman was pointing into the camera. A call to arms, he bellowed.

7.

After supper, the president retreated to her childhood bedroom with a warm washcloth on her face. She dug into her duffle bag and pulled out the dress the guru had given her at the institute. The dress she had modeled for him on that final day, feeling they were crossing some line. She brought it with her wherever she went, just like the pink-plated pistol. She twirled in front of the mirror like she had for the guru below the convention center. Then she started crying and tried to pop the pimple.

The head was drooping and bulbous—mushroom-like—but the tip had never turned white. Not ready, her mother said. But she had to do something. Her nostrils were drooping now too. Her nose grew longer as she squeezed it, the skin feeling thick in her hands. Why didn't it hurt? she wondered. She got lightheaded whenever she messed with it, but it almost felt good. With one hand she pressed down on the base, and with the other, tried to squeeze out the insides. She moved her hand in stiff jerks from her face—out toward the tip, squeezing as hard as she could. Her nose turned blood-red, her breathing heavy. She could feel it getting close, the pressure building, the tip huge and dark and angry.

After panting and moaning for half an hour, she finally managed to pop it. Her nose exploded in a milky white mess all over the mirror, and she screamed in surprise.

Then collapsed to her bed laughing, her legs weak and shaking, her neck and shoulders going soft. Are you OK? her mother asked outside the door.

Yes, the president answered, pulling the covers over herself. I'm fine. Bad dream. Don't come in. She listened to the whisper of footsteps on the carpet, feeling strange and empty and close to falling asleep.

Her mother was right. She had too much on her plate. Her limbs loose and tingly, she rolled from bed, hysterical, a laugh rising in the back of her throat. In the bathroom, she wadded up toilet paper to clean the mirror, and noticed that her panties were wet. Slimy. Her privates slick to the touch.

She laughed out loud by accident and remembered the guru coaching her before her big debate. You're on the edge, he had said whenever she got worked up. Pay attention now. Her nose had deflated significantly. It still hung there, flaccid, but hopefully it was on the mend. She was proud of herself and felt somehow stronger.

Back in her bedroom, though, it wasn't so funny. As she wiped down the mirror and changed her panties, she was struck with the idea that God had been watching her. She felt suddenly very small and started talking to herself.

I didn't mean to, she said, looking at her bare legs in the mirror. Sex sneaking in through a blemish. She fingered her promise ring, wanting suddenly to smash the mirror and cut off her nose so she wouldn't have to look at it anymore. After she changed into her PJs, she saw her wet panties on the floor and lost her breath thinking about her father finding them there.

She stuffed everything into the duffle bag and jumped into bed. But after a while, she got up, turned the mirror to face the wall, and plugged in the old nightlight. The corner of the room glowed pink as she prayed.

8.

It was worse back at school. It kept growing larger, hanging down around her lips now, obstructing her speech. Her nostrils clogged and puffed up like plums. She was too embarrassed to go to a doctor. She started wrapping a black scarf around her head. When she was mistaken at the campus chapel for a Muslim, she didn't correct the old woman at the desk who gave her the evil eye. Apparently, it made her angry too—these foreigners usurping Christian space in the name of liberal evenhandedness. She prayed silently in a pew afterward, worrying that her pale hands might give her away. She didn't want the old lady to soften up. They were both Christian soldiers in the Lord's service.

She stopped going to classes, made a fortress of her dorm room where only the puppy dog boy came to beg for help. Things had blown up at the pro-life table since the video, hundreds of students crowding round. It was on the nightly news.

Man-up, she told him through the cracked door. I can't do everything around here.

It was torture to unwrap the scarf in the evenings, torture to see the thing flop across her mouth. After her shower in the shared bathroom, she walked to the mirror in her room like a criminal to the chopping block. Nervous, playing with the promise ring on her finger, she always told herself this was the last time. That she would finally empty it completely. Her nose growing heavy in anticipation—pulsing with her heartbeat. Longer, thicker. Her nipples hard. She didn't want to do it, she told herself, squeezing her thighs together. She just wanted it to go away.

But every night she made a liar of herself, panting and shaking before the mirror. If she could just empty it, if she could get it all out, then maybe things would go back to normal.

9.

It must have been the Community Director—the one that wouldn't give her the A/C unit—that wrote the anonymous letter. Who else would have seen the boy in the lobby every night? Headed up the stairs to the president's room? It was going viral.

Dear readers, the letter opened, *I'm not one to go poking my nose into other people's business, but the current debate sweeping my campus and the nation at large reeks of hypocrisy. I think I smell a rat. Does this future first lady practice what she preaches? I have news for her celibate fans out there.*

Although the letter never directly said the president was having sex with the boy—never, in fact, even named the president—the article was crystal clear in its implications. It didn't matter which pieces were true or false. It was all about the way things looked. The image is all that matters, the guru always said. She remembered the outcry against fake news during the last election cycle. Liberal crybabies whining about the radioman and his network when they were guilty of the exact same thing. Media literacy. No one knew what it was. This anonymous letter was a smear campaign. She would have to change the optics. Change the conversation. She wrote a response about the virtue of chastity and the promise ring her father had given her. Took the chance to plug the Future First Ladies. No press is bad press, they say. She denied it all and maligned the anonymous writer as a coward for not signing her name. No balls, her supporters wrote in the comment sections. No balls on the liberal left.

Her father called to ask if she was OK. If there was any truth to the letter.

You've got to be kidding me! she said.

Calm down, he reassured her. I'm just checking on you.

It's bullshit, she cried, her eyes welling up. She looked at herself in the mirror. I don't know why they're doing this to me.

He told her she should get some rest, offered again to come and stay with her.

She could handle herself, she said.

These people are animals, her father insisted. They'll say anything to ruin a girl like you. He joked about where she should aim if any young men did come a-courting. Please be careful, he said. Sometimes we feel like we're losing you.

10.

The day before the planned protest at the chapel, she sent an email to the College Conservatives, letting them know that she couldn't attend. The coverage has been too much about me, she wrote, rather than what we stand for. She called for revolution not reform and requested that a female come and pick up the protest signs that she had been working on all week. A female, she made abundantly clear.

And a female came. But the boy was on her heels. He called first to tell the president something terrible had happened. That he had to see her in person to explain.

What happened? she asked. Just tell me over the phone.

Once again, it seemed, someone had stolen the dead baby posters from the quad. Safe spaces and micro traumas, micro aggressions in medical photos, it wasn't about the posters themselves, she shouted, but the principle of the damned thing. They were being stamped out by a generation of pussies who cheered for the murder of children.

They ran up, the boy explained, wearing rubber Richard Nixon masks—idiots thinking they were in a movie—and snatched the posters and ran off toward the bell tower. He gave chase, he said. But they were athletes—women from the track team, maybe basketball players—and they outran him easily.

She swore—which was very out of character.

And he apologized again. Then explained that although he didn't get a good look at the assailants, he was pretty sure they were black.

That doesn't matter, she answered, obviously annoyed. That's why people jump all over us. For saying stuff like that. She sounded like she was underwater.

He laughed. Of course it matters, he said. If we want to catch them, we have to know what they look like, don't we?

She started to interrupt him, but he talked over her. I filed a campus police report, he said. The boys in blue are behind us. *They* asked *me* about race. Not the other way around. He paused. You're not going PC on me, are you?

She didn't answer.

Talk to me! he said. I'm just kidding with you.

She thought about him clinging to her hand on their date and wondered if she would ever be pretty again. She imagined this thing flopping across his face when he tried to kiss her. The towel slipped down around her waist, and she stared at her breasts. Then at the pale skin below her belly button where her stomach slid away from her hipbones. Her nose began to throb.

I'm coming over, he said.

No, she answered, gathering up the towel. You can't.

It's too late, he said. I'm already here.

A tap-tap-tapping on the dorm room door, just behind the naked girl.

Stop, she said into the phone. Stop it. But he had already hung up.

I just want to talk to you, he whispered from the other side of the door.

No, she answered. Please. Go away.

I'm going to get louder and louder, he said.

Don't, she answered, opening the door.

I climbed up the outside of the stairwell, he said. Don't worry. No one saw me. He was breathing heavily. Why aren't you coming to the protest tomorrow?

She hid behind the door, the pistol on the desk beside her. I'll be there in spirit, she said.

That doesn't mean anything, he answered. You planned it, and we need you there. His voice was desperate. Why won't you let me see you?

I don't think it's a good idea, she answered. You know what I've got back here.

He could see a fraction of her room behind the door, the mirror smeared with some type of residue, her panties balled up on the floor. His breath caught in his throat.

Shoot me, then, he said. I don't care. We need you there tomorrow.

Soon, she answered, closing the door. Soon everything will be back to normal.

11.

She was out at sunrise the next day. Anonymous in her headscarf and gloves, her black pants and turtleneck. Spy in the belly of the beast, soldier of the Lord, invisible and shapely, silent in her tennis shoes. She cut through the quad, hid behind the science building, watched the boy shuffling from the union with the table. He had a freshman recruit helping him out. It's pitiful, if you think about it, he told the new boy. The poster was just one tool for changing hearts and minds. It doesn't really matter. We'll have a new one by next week, no problem.

But don't you want revenge? asked the other boy.

Of course, her friend answered, but it's the principle that matters.

The president smiled to herself.

I get it, the other boy said. But it's hard to always be the bigger man.

Sure is, her friend answered. But it's all about the image. If they weren't screaming about it, we'd know we were doing something wrong.

She almost laughed to hear her words in his mouth. The scarf was coming unhitched, her nose growing larger. She tried to sneak away while it was still manageable, but she dropped her phone on the brick walkway as she stood up.

Both boys turned and saw her running away.

You better run, yelled the unfamiliar one. You dirty fucking towelhead.

Behind the library, she collapsed into a rhododendron thicket on the edge of the arboretum and began sobbing. No matter how hard she willed it to shrink, her nose throbbed to her heartbeat as the sun came up. Warm light through the waxy evergreen, she went cross-eyed staring at it. Unmistakable. She felt the old hysterical tightening, couldn't tell if she was laughing or crying. Give it air. She heard her mother's voice. Don't mess. She closed her eyes and prayed for help. Pay attention. You're on the edge.

She had no idea how long she had been there when her phone rang. Breaking the trance of her anxious prayer. People's legs swished by on the walkways all around her, and she silenced her phone so that no one would find her in the bush. It was her father, the screen of her phone flashing DADDY, until the voicemail kicked in. He left a short message. Then texted her afterward. Apparently, there were pictures on the internet. She had no idea what he was talking about. *Out there for the whole world to see*, his text read.

She sat hunched in the bush, the thing on her face still long and hard and aching as she swiped through the internet news sites. They all had the story. Pictures of the boy climbing up the outside of the concrete stairwell. How was this news? His hand on the knob of her dorm room door—still spray-painted, unmistakable. It was an invasion of her privacy. The door opening. It was pornography. In the last picture, the door was closed again and the boy nowhere in sight, the narrative obvious in its implications. He had come to spend the night. There were timestamps on the photos and another anonymous letter. *I hate that it's come to this,* the letter read. *But I must vindicate myself in the face of hypocrisy.*

She went numb in the dirt, her world falling to pieces. The past and the future fading away. She lost herself in the polished leaves. She couldn't feel a thing. Netted in the dappled light of the rhododendron. Floating. Her hand drifted to her face, and she stroked it slowly, felt the blood rushing in the veins. Then harder. Her joints loose, she lost all sense of direction, closed her eyes, felt that she was upside down. Kaleidoscope of green beneath the umbrella shrub. She smelled flowers though she couldn't smell a thing, tasted honey. Felt her hand down her pants—shaped like a pistol—hot and slick.

Until she exploded in a wave of silver and melted into the earth. Breathless. Flower petals dewy, the buzz and hum of sunlight in the bush.

There were denim legs and tennis shoes when she opened her eyes, the shadows of torsos towering over the shrub. She fumbled out from beneath it, already running, choking, through the garden toward the chapel, away from the laughter, the scarf streaming from her face like a skinny black flag.

12.

They had tried to force the Quran down her throat as a freshman. The text of terrorists, of jihad, of war against the West. Required reading for a state university. Ring, freedom, ring. Protesting against this abuse of power had been her first act as a College Conservative. She vowed to keep to the fringe this time, to let others take the reins.

But the scene at the chapel when she arrived was more than she had bargained for. Hundreds of people crowded into the plaza in front of the old Gothic church, and there were news vans parked on the sidewalks with their satellite antennas stretching skyward. Metal barricades snaked across the flagstones to separate the protesters from one another, and people on both sides were already shouting. She saw the College Conservatives out front, some waving signs that she herself had made, and she started walking toward them without thinking.

There were other conservative groups too, some with their faces painted, some waving American flags. All of them shouting at the Muslim Coalition and their liberal allies on the other side. The newscasters stood in between, talking into their microphones. She thought of her father watching in his armchair, Mary Todd in his lap. She touched the promise ring on her finger and almost cried.

Seek forgiveness, he had said on her voicemail. You've proven yourself a liar.

But this was the place to change hearts and minds. Right here. In front of the cameras. The image, the guru said, is all that really matters. She felt a red glow in her chest. But as she walked over the flagstones—through the blank space between the warring factions—she suddenly realized that a man in a turban was yelling at her.

Where are you going? he shouted. You're headed the wrong way.

A deer in the headlights, she tried to move in both directions at once. All alone in the middle. The newscasters turned toward her, and everything went silent.

Come back over here, the man in the turban yelled again.

Everyone was watching.

She felt their eyes on her body. The scarf began to tighten, and before she could think, she shook her head at the man. No, she answered. Throwing a thumb over her shoulder. I'm with them, she said, turning toward the conservative crowd. Her feet hardly touched the ground—past the news cameras—the conservatives erupting in applause.

The perfect visual, a woman in a headscarf strolling away from the angry left—into the open arms of the cheering right. The chapel rising immaculate behind her. Holy politics—here—in front of God's house. Every step, a thunderbolt, worth a thousand words.

Her own College Conservatives were cheering louder than anyone else. The lovesick boy looked into her eyes and smiled. She winked at him. He grabbed her hand and raised it into the air. On wings from above, she turned to face the cameras and felt lightheaded, lifted.

Before realizing something was terribly wrong.

A voice was screaming behind her. Over here, it said, you gotta lose the scarf.

She clutched at her face and her friend tried to fight off whoever it was that had grabbed her. Scuffle, scuffle, someone cursed. People shouted. Stop. What are you doing? Others began chanting, Lose the scarf.

Her head jerked backwards from the force. The scarf unraveled in a flash, pulled up and away in an explosion of blonde hair. Everyone silent for just a moment, so that the slap of the thing swinging down upon her lips rung out like the clap of a bell. Her scream tore through the silence like bullets. Like a woman giving birth in the wilderness. And long after the scarf was pulled into the collapsing crowd, she still grabbed at the thing that had veiled her from the world.

13.

Within minutes, the image shot to the top of every social media newsfeed. Political pundits began weighing in before the police had even dispersed the crowd. Opinions streamed across the internet like tessellating birds in flight.

After apparently imitating a Muslim woman in a headscarf, the Branch President of the College Conservatives (President of Students for Life, Founder and President of the Future First Ladies, graduate of the guru's famous institute, campaigner for the doctor politician, congregant of the good reverend, sometimes surrogate for the radioman himself, a girl famous for viral videos) stood in full relief in front of her own organization this afternoon—and a hundred likeminded conservative protestors—for a truly blasphemous unveiling.

Snap-snap-snap went the cameras as the scarf unraveled, everyone holding their breath as the blonde hair burst—almost white in the sun—the girl throwing her hands up like a child. The stone monolith of the bright chapel behind her, the dancing worshiper, up on her tiptoes like a ballerina, desperate and all alone in front of the barricade.

There was a penis in the middle of her face where her nose should have been, pulled up by the tug of the scarf, levitating in a bulbous glob, then—in what seemed slow motion—flopping down across her lips. A resounding clap ringing out as she shrieked and fell to her knees. Snap-snap-snap, the thing swinging like the tongue of a bell against her face. Heavy. Before chaos broke loose and the barricades fell.

14.

Trampled in the clash, she lay pinned beneath a metal fence, a whimpering creature—hermaphroditic—forgotten. Suffocating among the boots and tennis shoes. Hysterical. The puppy dog boy wrenched her free at some point and dragged her through the yellow tear-gas clouds, through the bodies grappling and the sobbing women, her arms limp, her legs stumbling along. He sat her down beside an azalea bush. Tried to pull the prosthetic penis from her face. Did you glue it on? he asked her, smiling. Trying to hide that pimple?

But when the thing began growing hard in his hands, he jumped back. Afraid. He said something about revolution. Retreated into the crowd, throwing strange looks over his shoulder, his fists above his head, a question in his eyes.

She was gone when he returned, and there was a little puddle of milky fluid on the bricks where she had been sitting. He wanted to go looking for her, but he didn't dare try her dorm room. Not after the pictures from the night before. She might shoot him, after all. Even more controversy to come with this prank. How poignant. The meaning obvious, he thought. But what would the pundits say?

He cut a shortcut through the quad to check on the pro-life table, playing over in his head the way she had winked at him from within the scarf. He loved her more than anything, he thought. The torch of conservatism burned brightly in her steady hands. The two of them would carry it forward together. Beneath the bronze statues of Confederate men, he wondered what image they themselves might leave for the generations that would follow in their footsteps.

15.

She bandaged herself as best she could before heading home. A splint on her wrist, a roll of gauze wrapped around her face like a mummy. She was surprised when her father opened the door instead of her mother. His face as cold as the granite facade of the chapel.

She couldn't catch her breath and felt the blood rushing to her face. Her nose engorged and growing thick before her eyes. When she noticed the pale loop on his finger where his promise ring had been, she started crying. Right there on the doorstep.

Somewhere far away she heard a violin like a woman's voice and tasted tiramisu.

I'm disappointed, he said. But I know you're going through a lot, so we can wait and talk about it later. He stepped back to permit her entrance, and she shuffled inside with her head hung low, blonde curls poking through the gauze.

I feel sorry for you, he said, as she mounted the stairs. But God is gracious. He'll forgive you if you ask.

She mumbled something he couldn't understand. Her voice unclear, muzzled, choked in the gauze. He almost called out as she reached the landing, her pink duffle bag bouncing behind her. But his voice caught in his throat. Instead, he wandered through the living room, staring at framed family photos on the wall. *Spare the rod and spoil the child*, the good book says. Personal responsibility. He looked at the pale loop on his finger and shook his head, wondering what he might have done differently. And never considered for a moment the gravity of that other gift: the pink-plated pistol that had bounced up the carpeted steps behind his daughter.

Consubstantial

Today we can almost physically hear the mutterings and rumblings of an invigorated god of war.

The one encouraging thing is that the mad moment has not yet arrived for the firing of the gun or the exploding of the bomb which will set civilization about the final task of destroying itself. There is still a hope for peace if we finally decide that no longer can we safely blind our eyes and close our ears to those facts which are shaping up more and more clearly—and that is that we are now engaged in a show-down fight—not the usual war between nations for land area or other material gains, but a war between two diametrically opposed ideologies.

The great difference . . . is not political, gentlemen, it is moral. . . .

The real, basic difference . . . lies in the religion of immoralism. . . . [I]f the ***RED*** *half of the world triumphs—and well it may, gentlemen—this religion of immoralism will more deeply wound and damage mankind than any conceivable economic or political system.*

Today we are engaged in a final, all-out battle. . . . [T]he chips are down—they are truly down.

Ladies and gentlemen, can there be anyone tonight who is so blind as to say that the war is not on? Can there be anyone who fails to realize that . . . the time is now—that this is the time for the show-down between the . . . Christian world and the . . . atheistic world?

Unless we face this fact, we shall pay the price that must be paid by those who wait too long. . . .

. . . As one of our outstanding historical figures once said, "When a great democracy is destroyed, it will not be from enemies from without, but rather because of enemies from within."

The reason why we find ourselves in a position of impotency is . . . because of the traitorous actions of those who have been treated so well by this Nation. . . .

He has lighted the spark which is resulting in a moral uprising and will end only when the whole sorry mess of twisted, warped thinkers are swept from the national scene so that we may have a new birth of honesty and decency in government.

—United States Senator Joseph McCarthy

On a bright June day, the radioman exited the brick box of a building where he had just completed another successful episode. He whistled as he walked, his eyes hidden behind his sunglasses, thinking about how quickly the pills had killed the pain. He'd have to get more from the doctor, he thought. The black leather wingtips on his feet flashed in the sun. He stood as straight as an arrow. Like a man half his age, he thought, nodding toward a big-breasted woman bouncing past. Now that Martha was gone, it wouldn't even be cheating, he thought.

Two months of hell: gone at the snap of his fingers. The rattling of a bottle. He hadn't been able to sleep at night, his body twisted beneath the sheets like an arthritic claw. Like Martha's mother's feet jutting from the hospital bed. Martha's feet starting to look the same. It was those feet as much as anything that sent him to the doctor. Only so many years left, he reasoned. The doctor wrote a prescription, and just like that, he was done with the strapped-on brace, the orthopedic chair, the bi-weekly trips to the chiropractor.

Two years since the trouble with the press. Mainstream media accusing him of abuse. Martha promising to leave him if he ever touched the pills again. At least the old bird stayed true to her word. It wasn't his fault, however, that the doctor botched the job. The medication had been prescribed, after all, and the past two years without it had been a nightmare.

He stood in line at the 7-Eleven behind blonde teenagers. A boy and a girl with the same length hair, her butt-cheeks hanging from her shorts. What class, he thought, as they kissed in front of him, their pink tongues stretching into one another's mouths. Cigarettes behind their ears, a case of beer between their feet. The world gone to hell in a handbasket, he thought. And whose cash was that on the counter? Their parents? When he was their age, he'd had a job. He almost told them so. The boy pointed to a pack of condoms on the wall behind the register, and the attendant reached up and grabbed them. Absurd. The radioman imagined himself a fiery angel of justice.

They turned—the boy's hand still gripping her butt—and swaggered through the sliding glass door like they owned the world.

Did you ID them? the radioman asked the attendant.

Yes, sir, the attendant answered. A little stubby man with flaky skin. Must pick at himself, thought the radioman.

I didn't see it.

They come in every day, sir. I know them.

They didn't look it.

No sir, but they are. I promise. How can I help you?

They buy beer and condoms every day?

The attendant shrugged. Yes sir, he said.

Jesus Christ. The radioman shook his head. So, you know what they're up to, then?

The attendant smirked. I could wager a guess, he said.

Trying to control his anger, the radioman shook his head. I'll take your finest cigar, he said.

Purple wrapper, aromatic. He walked back into the sun, trying to forget this oasis in the desert, this cool den of sex with sliding doors. He'd had girls like her since Martha. Mirages on the horizon. During Martha. As young and blonde as her, though he couldn't recall their faces. What would their fathers think? He imagined catching the couple in the act and tearing them to pieces like an animal.

The streets were empty at midday, and he was thankful there was no one to recognize him. He thought about the show they'd just finished recording. The ratings as high as ever. People were angry about the world's decay, about teenagers with condoms and beer. People weren't going to take it anymore.

The trick was to catch them young. Like that pretty little thing from the university who filled in for him when he was sick. National head of Students for Life. She was doing the good Lord's work. Superstar on the horizon. Easier to convince people with legs like hers.

Poor Martha. The medicine made him nostalgic. She was never coming back. He struck a match and recalled the stubby fingers of the gas station attendant. Like the hands of that doctor holding their blue baby all those years ago. What a creature, he thought. Grinning from his plastic cage. Surrounded by cigarettes and lotto tickets and condoms for little boys. Forget about it, he told himself. It's a sweet-smelling dandy of a day, and you're the face of the moral majority.

His shoulders back, he felt bodily lifted, hanging on a wire from heaven. His leather wingtips clicked past dog walkers and young mothers pushing strollers, past young men and women jogging and kids skidding around on skateboards. To the bench beneath the oak tree that looked out on the lake. The women in spandex bounced past, beneath the sun like golden angels.

He jolted his spine when he plopped himself down and shook two more pills from the bottle. Relax, he told himself. Don't exceed the daily dosage. He puffed on the cigar, assuring himself he didn't have enough to abuse.

Have to get more, he thought, watching a lady in a dollar-green sports bra jiggle along the path. Clothes probably pop when you peel them off, he thought. *Lecherous* was the word they'd use. But he could still get it up. There's a pill for that too. Martha said it went against nature. He crossed one leg over the other, leaned back on the bench, and watched the cigar smoke dissipate into the leaves. No spunk left in the old gal, he thought. But he was still young enough to sire a child. To start over again.

Dappled sunlight fell through the canopy, languorous. The jogging ladies moved to the slow vibrations of the world. Rebounding and rubbery. Something he might gobble up. He felt the heartbeat of America. Felt drowsy in the heat.

One too many, he thought, bolting upright. He felt his bones loosen. The world faded to green. Action, though, was what got him into trouble. *Violent* was the word they used. It was better to sleep it off. How many had he taken? The women bounced into the air and swam through the leaves. He'd have to ask the doctor for more.

*

No one saw him in the shadows, the leaf-filtered sunlight dancing on his pink face. As he slumped to the side, his hat fell from his head. Then his cigar from his mouth—onto the cedar chips scattered around the tree. Aromatic, evaporating to ash. Now resting in the cocoon of the gray-veined brown leaf. Now blown by the whisper of evening wind. He didn't move in his sleep, part and parcel of the bench as the sun dipped below the trees, coloring the ground golden, throwing long shadows into the park. Fading.

Then gone. He slept. The park emptied with the sunlight, the iron lamps at intervals blinked to life. Headlights swept over the grass, and traffic hummed on the other side of the low stone wall. Past suppertime, lone joggers in the dark moved swift and faceless.

When at last he woke up, it was with a start. As if he knew he shouldn't have been there.

Stars speckled the sky beyond the tree. And as he blinked himself back into being, he realized he wasn't alone on the bench.

He jumped to his feet, his legs wobbly beneath him. A very young man in a very white suit sat calmly atop the wooden slats, adjusting his tie with his long white fingers, his hair parted to the side and slicked back—black—a faint mustache above his very pink lips. He looked familiar. The radioman rubbed his eyes and stared.

Who are you? he asked, still sleepy and stuttering as he stared at the other man's lips.

The stranger pulled a white handkerchief from the breast pocket of his white suit. He dabbed at his mouth. His suit seemed to glow in the dark. He smirked as if they shared some secret. He tucked the handkerchief back into his pocket.

Those were quite the moves, he said with a wink.

What do you mean? the radioman asked. He looked around to see if anyone else was there. The whole world moved in slow motion.

The other laughed. His breath smelled sweet. I said, those were quite the moves. He adjusted the handkerchief, a bloom of white on white. I didn't know an old queer like you could still get it up, he said. He raised his eyebrows. And both ways too. Very democratic of you.

What did you do? asked the radioman. He could hear his own voice far away. It sounded like someone else's.

Laughter bubbled beneath the penciled mustache. It smelled of lavender—a purple sprig—in the warm night air. You tell yourself whatever you want, honey, the man said. I'm not here to judge. He winked and rose from the bench. He almost seemed to float. But I wouldn't be opposed to doing it again, he said, his hips gyrating. And again, and again.

Get out of here, you faggot, yelled the radioman. He swung wildly at the other, lost his balance, fell into the cedar chips.

The stranger leapt nimbly away, lacing his long white fingers above his heart as if he was hurt. Don't be a sourpuss, he said, batting his lashes. I know how sweet you really are. He slid his hands down his body until he cradled his crotch in his fingers. As sweet as they come, he said, raising his eyebrows and giggling. His breath smelled of flowers.

Why you little—. The radioman rushed him, his hands outstretched. But again, his legs gave way.

Sweeter than sweet, the stranger said, darting behind the oak tree. He played peekaboo like a child, his face on one side, then the other. Like honey on the tongue. He was a vanishing white wisp. As sweet as they come. A twist of smoke, then nothing, just the smell of lavender in the air. I'll see you soon, papa bear. His voice like an echo down a long hallway. Then gone.

The radioman stood up holding his head. His breath was hard to catch, he put his hands on his knees. His belt was undone, his pants unbuttoned and drooping past his thighs. Pervert, he said. What did that little pervert do?

The shadows vibrated with his heavy breathing. He could feel the cigar in his lungs. Cloudy. Up into his head. Was he dreaming? Lamplight and stars, the tree like a great umbrella. The bench beneath it—perfectly squat and still, lit up like a bulb—his hat sitting on top of it. There was a faint pain in his belly.

He checked behind the tree, then ran wildly onto the path. Hello? he cried. Hello?

He must look crazy, he thought, hollering like that. He saw Martha's looming face. Disappointed. Their son would have been about the age of that stranger.

There'd be trouble if someone saw him now. News stories, flashing bulbs, the threat of termination. He took a deep breath, leaned on an iron lamp post, checked again to make sure he was alone. Hallucinations after the operation. Botched job. He felt underwater again.

Too many, he whispered, shaking the bottle in his pocket. He tied his shoe and put his ballcap on. He took deep breaths, found his balance, hustled from the park holding onto the dull ache in his stomach.

*

Two weeks later the doctor told him he couldn't refill the prescription.

Why? he asked, sitting on the padded bench, trying to peek at his chart.

The doctor swiveled in the chair until he was looking at him. You already know, don't you? he asked.

The radioman shook his head. Since that night at the park, he'd been very careful about spacing out the pills. He shrugged his shoulders. I have no idea, he said.

Really? the doctor asked, taking off his glasses. You haven't noticed anything?

The radioman shook his head again.

Well, the doctor said, clapping his hands together. It's good news. He loosened his tie.

The radioman stared back at him, confused. How could it be good if he wasn't getting what he'd come for? He would have to change doctors again, he thought, looking at the man's stubby fingers.

You're pregnant! the doctor said. The smile frozen on his face.

They sat and stared at each other in silence, the radioman scowling at him, the doctor beaming back. Surprise!

Slowly, a smile crept onto the radioman's face. He laughed. Chuckling at first, then louder and louder. The doctor laughed with him, both of them cracking up in the little white room. The radioman slapped his thigh and reached out to shake the doctor's hand. Their eyes teared up, and water ran down their faces, until a nurse poked her head into the room.

Is everything all right? she asked.

They nodded at her. Unable to stop. Until she started giggling as well and said, OK, and shut the door.

When they finally caught their breath, the doctor had the hiccups.

Jesus, doc! The radioman chuckled. You're a real cutup. Pregnant!

The doctor's hand was slippery in his own, but he held on tight. I'll tell you what, he continued. My back really has been *killing* me, and I'd appreciate another prescription.

The doctor pulled his hand away, a question in his eyes. He put his glasses on and glanced at the chart again. I can't give you any more pills, he said. You're pregnant.

The scene that followed culminated in the radioman being thrown from the office like a drunk from a bar. Get out, they said, and stay out. The glass door snapping closed behind him. The security guard crossing his arms over his chest.

He shouldn't have gotten so worked up, he admitted to himself. But why did the doctor have to joke like that? A simple no would have done the trick. A scolding. A lecture on self-control. Martha's language. The therapist's. But the pain was real, goddamn it!

People stared at him in the parking lot, their phones in their hands. Were they recording him? Déjà vu as he ran toward his car. Doctor's office, ambulance ride, mug shot, front page, nightly news, public recovery, bullshit.

It could all fall apart, he thought, trying to hide his face as he swerved from the parking lot. Everyone wanted him to fail.

Get you hooked, rat you out, wash their hands. Good riddance, he thought, you'll not crucify me. White coats—clean—shifting blame to the patient. Not again, he thought. Not this time.

*

Weeks passed. The ratings went up. There was a TV deal in the works.

It's about time they put this pretty mug on camera, he said, smiling after the show. The secretaries giggled, their breasts bouncing as they laughed. He vowed to take one of them out to dinner before Christmas. It was about time, wasn't it? They were all so fertile looking. He saw Martha's frowning face breaking to pieces. Nightmares of miscarriage.

He popped aspirin like candy, telling himself it was good for his heart. One of the temps was doing his damnedest to get ahold of something stronger. He'd promised the boy a full-time job if he came through with the drugs. It's a good job, he told him. The launching ground for politicians. A beacon of hope in this wasteland. Yes, the boy answered. You're the voice of America, doing the good Lord's work.

You should run for office, the callers said. We'd vote for you. You'd win.

He laughed into the microphone. If I ran, he said, who would do my job?

The staff applauded in the office afterward. You're one of a kind, they said.

The old anger in his voice again. Growling back after all these years.

Changes inside the brick box of a building. Back to the material that made him great.

Changes outside, as well. He drank scotch in the evening to get to sleep and woke up sick in the morning. Bent over the toilet bowl, trying to purge the fleeting dreams. The man in the white suit touching himself, his cock jutting through the teeth of his zipper. Wisps of lavender smoke, pink tongues, blue babies. He stood naked in the bathroom mirror, flashbacks to somewhere, to something. Naked. Martha's shaking head. The allegations piling up. Yes, there had been other women. Everything fuzzy back then.

Afternoons in the park, trying to calm himself down. He sat on the bench under the oak tree, smoking cigars, watching women. The sunlight shimmered on the pond. He never saw the man again. Wingtips clicking down the sidewalk, the sound not as sharp, the shine not as bright. His back curved in a slump, his feet heavy in his angel shoes. His wire to heaven sagging. Beginning to shuffle the old man dance. But it wasn't yet time, he told himself. He could still sire a child, goddamn it. Those pills could make him into an acrobat, couldn't they? That's what the man in the white suit had said. A dream on a park bench, a scented cigar. His pants around his ankles.

He sometimes caught himself shouting at no one at all and had to hurry away from wherever he was. He couldn't shake the image of the stranger's handkerchief, the bloom of white on white.

*

Then his belly started growing. Slowly. He watched his wrinkled skin smooth out, the secretaries poking fun at him from behind their desks. Laugh it off, old man, he told himself. He ate fruit for breakfast, and veggies for lunch. What his father had always called *rabbit food*. Bounce like a bunny, he told himself.

But nothing seemed to help. Haggard, overworked, he grew bags under his eyes. Shuffled along, assuring himself this wasn't the first time he'd been fat. In the past, though, it was always the meds and the booze. The big appetite. Less work, late nights, Martha in distress. Never like this before. Home alone after work for a TV dinner and two glasses of scotch. Aspirin by the fistful for his back that knocked him breathless. His stomach aching, his throat sore from throwing up. Week after week after week.

It just kept growing, the pooch above his genitals in the bathroom mirror. His skin taut, his back even worse than in the old days. He remembered the botched job and the weeks that followed. When he first experienced the miracle of prescription pain pills. The cool slide. Careful, Martha said. Be careful with those.

Now he found himself hunched above his desk at work. Groaning when he got up to pee. People stopped and stared. Then gathered to gossip by the water cooler.

The bottle of aspirin rattled in his pocket. People knew when he was coming and got out of his way. Death rattle, he thought. Death shuffling through the office. It couldn't be good for his stomach, he thought. Pieces of his insides sloughing off in the morning. Into the toilet. He decided to see another doctor.

*

Two in a day, the same story repeated. Nonchalant in their white rooms, white men with pale hands, their faces scrubbed clean. They opened his chart and nodded their heads. Pregnant, their prognosis. Yes, pregnant, no doubt about it. It couldn't be more obvious, sir. No, they couldn't prescribe pain pills to someone who was expecting. Not the kind he was asking for, at least. Have you tried aspirin? He sat on the patient bench, smiling along with them. Come on, he said. You've got to be kidding me.

This is no joke, sir, they said. Is everything OK?

That I'm pregnant?

Yes, sir.

Of course not.

Then silence in the white rooms. One after the other. Concerned faces above their stethoscopes. Assholes. Keep cool, he told himself. He pointed at their charts. What did you write in there? he asked. Did y'all get together to mess with me? A bunch of shit-eating liberal Poindexters, he thought. Laughing while I'm suffering, he said. This isn't a fucking joke.

The doctors shook their heads. We can't prescribe you this medication until after you give birth.

Give birth? he shouted. I'm a man, goddamn it!

They looked down at their charts. Well, they said, laying heavy hands on his shoulders, the tests say what the tests say.

Would you like me to recommend an obstetrician? the second one asked.

The man's white lapels ended up in his fists. The doctor saying, Sir! Calm down.

I'll break him open, thought the radioman. Watch his insides spill on the floor. The nurses clawed at him, two, three, four. Sir, stop hitting him, they said. Please, sir, their faces crazy. Let him go.

*

The fourth doctor told him if he didn't want it there were other options and gave him the number of the abortion clinic. Scribbled digits on a white scrap, passed from hand to hand. You only have this option for so long, he said, his eyes glued to the radioman's bulging stomach. When did you start showing? he asked.

Showing? asked the radioman.

Yes, showing. Getting bigger.

He tried to count in his head. A few months, I guess, he answered.

Better act quick, the doctor advised. If not, there's always adoption.

The radioman stared at him, blank-faced, his hands atop his bald head.

I'm not here to judge, the doctor said. But once it starts kicking, you'll have to carry it to term. He shrugged his shoulders. Quickening, they call it. Not a state in the union you can flush it after that.

Flush it? the radioman asked.

That's not what I said.

The radioman called him a sick bastard.

Sir, the doctor answered. That's not what I said.

Cut-rate piece of shit, you're talking about a baby.

Listen, mister, you're the one who said—

Up and out of the office. He had to get out before he blew his top. In the parking lot, he tried to pull his coat tight, but it wouldn't button. His belly hung from the bottom of his shirt. He saw himself in car windows as he passed, a stranger. Been showing how long? He tried to take deep breaths. Months now, he thought, the world spinning. Careening toward what?

He stared at his penis that night in the bathroom mirror. A short pink drooping between his legs. Pitiful. Made for beer and condoms in the summertime. For blonde babes with bouncing butt-cheeks. For making babies. Poor Martha. He remembered their son kicking inside her. His belly hung enormous below his bosom. He looked at his nipples. Imagined a child latched on.

Where was his wire to heaven? His whole body pulled in toward his stomach now. Shoulders slouching, chest sagging, butt-cheeks sucked inward. His privates like the little knot tied below a balloon. How could anything come out of that?

*

Another month passed. He was hungry all the time. Everyone agreed he needed a vacation.

Take all the time you need, boss. You've been great.

Waddling down the hallway, he anticipated furtive glances. All of them snickering behind their hands. None of them loyal, he thought, a generation of slackers. Wasted. The country gone to hell.

The temp who had tried to get him the drugs followed him into the elevator. The radioman tried to remember his name. Too little, too late, he thought, glancing around the metal cell. I got some more, the boy said as the elevator doors slid closed, his fist clenched tight around something.

The radioman stared at him. He shook his head and smiled. You have to get *some* before you get *more*, he said.

The boy's blue eyes locked with his. He looked confused as he shook his hair from his face. But I already gave you—

The radioman cut him off. It's alright, son, don't sweat it. You got your job, didn't you?

Yes, sir, but—

Don't worry about it. You tried. He took the boy's hand. One quick rattling shake as they dinged down the floors one by one. Then they both put their hands in their pockets and stared at their reflections in the elevator's doors. When the radioman exited, he felt compelled to say something, so he blurted out—Keep up the good work, son.

The boy's empty hands hung at his sides. He mumbled, Thank you, sir. And God bless America.

Too bad, thought the radioman. Out of the brick box of a building. He turned his collar up against the cold and wondered if he'd ever come back. The aspirin rattling in his pocket, he popped the top and shook some into his mouth. Amphibious, he thought. A cartoon monster. His car leaned sideways when he sat down in the driver's seat and squeezed his bloated stomach beneath the steering wheel. He cursed and pulled the lever to recline the seat.

Cursed as he pulled out of the parking lot. Martha hated language like that. He was an island bulging from himself. Smoke in the rearview, wisps of rubber, disappearing like the man in the white suit.

That wasn't me on the bench, he thought. I wasn't myself. I'm still dreaming.

Past the 7-Eleven, cool den of sex. He imagined that boy's hand—a snake's mouth—latched onto the meat of the girl's butt. He imagined smashing the attendant's face. The park rolling green on the other side. He'd missed his chance to have a girl like that. The oak tree spread wide so God couldn't see beneath it. That man in the white suit, a virus. He remembered the AIDS updates he'd done on his show during the epidemic a lifetime ago. Bad taste, good ratings. Making jokes about the disease. Now look at him. What had that faggot done to him?

How? he shouted, punching his stomach. How? He popped another pill.

And then he felt it kick.

And the world broke to pieces.

Terror crossed his face. A shadow. He saw fractals spinning all around him. No, he thought. It can't be. He met his own eyes in the rearview mirror. The car floated through the winter sunlight. A man levitated above a park bench. Wait, he said. Once it starts kicking—. Everything went silent. The world seemed to wait along with him.

Until it happened again.

Something tapping inside. It couldn't be.

He knew where the clinic was. He'd boycotted there in the eighties and nineties, the aughts, with fire in his throat. A small-time disk jockey—angry, radical, red—a radioboy blossoming into *the* radioman. If only Martha had been able. She'd always wanted children.

He felt a stab of pain in his belly and swallowed more pills. How? he shouted. They rattled down his throat. All they'd ever wanted was a child. And all those people at the clinic, flushing God's greatest blessing! The greatest genocide the world's ever seen.

*

He swerved into the parking lot, wondering how he'd gotten there so fast. The blue and white lettering enormous. So that country girls wouldn't get lost, he had once heard a man joke. Inside, animals ate their own young. He suddenly wondered why he was there. Slip in, slip out. Ghosts in white rooms, ghosts in white jackets. Slip in, slip out. Children in trash bags, dumped into dumpsters. Vanished in a puff of smoke, the hum of a vacuum cleaner.

He scraped the front bumper on the concrete divider, the metal undercarriage like nails on a chalkboard. Undercarriage, aftercarriage, afterbirth, miscarriage. Martha. The whole world spilling out of her. He struggled from the car, cussing, red-faced, and waddled through the parking lot, listening to his wingtips. Click-click, like hooves scuffing the ground, his swollen feet bulging the black leather. Devil man. He couldn't catch his breath.

Grunting animal toward a den of animals. Papa bear. That's what the man in the white suit had called him. Papa. Up the steps, the sun too bright, and through the door. All eyes on him. He wanted to burn the place down.

Beelining toward the receptionist behind the little window in the wall, shouting—Get it out of me.

She was terrified—her mouth agape. Get it out! he shouted, the world spinning away from him. Christ! Help me, he hollered. I can't do it!

He whipped around before she could answer. He lurched into the waiting room, wondering why he'd come. Killers with their hands in their laps. That boy in the corner with the blonde hair, a cigarette behind his ear, how predictable. From the 7-Eleven to the abortion clinic. The girl back there with her legs spread familiar. A masked murderer poking her insides out.

Sir, the receptionist said again. Sir! Leaning from the little window. Sir, calm down. She communicated to the others with her hands. Tribe people. Sodomites, Gomorrahans, the room swam. Please, she yelled. You're scaring him.

The radioman's nostrils flared, his face bulged, he was there to bring blood. A prophet. An angel on winged feet with God's voice in his throat. I was lost, but now I'm found, he bellowed. He stomped back toward the little window, furious, standing straight as an arrow, feeling no pain. He was a beam of light buoyed by belief.

When he reached out for the receptionist, she slammed the window shut. Another nurse grabbed the phone and started punching numbers. Men in white suits gathered. Goddamned doctors stacked against him. Hacking women's insides to bits. A slaughter of the innocents.

Murderers, he shouted, not realizing he had broken the window in the wall until he heard the women screaming on the other side. His face straight through the shattered glass. Screaming. Fire fangs pulling at his flesh. Saying what? Was that his voice threatening them? Or someone else's far away? Blood everywhere, he thought. Martha in the bathroom crying.

He felt glass in his neck bone. But no pain. Full of the spirit. He pulled his head out, headfirst. A blue baby. Bye-bye. Hands wet, warm, blood-covered. Jesus, he couldn't see. Wondering where the door was, banging into walls. Everything caving in. Blunt instruments scraping insides. Spread legs. Where's the door? he shouted, throwing chairs across the room. Glass shattering. Let the air in. That's the way.

Light of day, light of God, he squeezed his body through the glass. Martha's insides spilling out. Now run, he thought, waddling toward his car. The blonde boy peeling out of the parking lot, afraid. Father exemplar fleeing the scene, men in white suits behind him. Come to get me, thought the radioman, with lavender on their breath. Fucking faggots. Never again, he shouted over his shoulder.

He had to catch the blonde boy. Teach him God's ways. Teach him to be the father that he had never been. But time was fleeting now. Quickening. Crusaders through the world—like father, like son—they would save this damned country or burn it down. Together. He couldn't keep his thoughts straight. That boy the same age his own boy would have been.

Pedal to the metal, he saw history laid out before him, a great orgy beneath an oak tree. We must do it together, he thought. Gaining on the boy's car. We'll bathe the world in fire, we'll fuck them till they die. He saw visions of himself wielding a great burning phallus, and for a moment wondered where he was going.

The devil, he shouted. Inside me. Bring crosses, burning. Holy men and heated clothes hangers. Let the light in. The world streamed by. There was blood in his eyes, the steering wheel slippery in his hands. He felt like his stomach might explode.

We'll go together, he thought, like father, like son. All the strings from heaven snapping, the sky falling. A blind streak down the asphalt, seeing visions of the afterlife, blue babies bouncing in clouds, penises sharpened like knives. Body bags in dumpsters, heaven on the other side. Pearly doors sliding open like an elevator. Stumpy St. Peter behind a cash register, punching numbers, a wall of condoms behind him. The blonde boy vanishing like a phantom. Like a snake. Like the baby in his belly. Crushed into the wheel. Wedged. A holocaust of children crying from the roadside.

Smoke rising all around him. He smelled lavender as he breathed and suddenly knew—beyond any doubt—that the man in the white suit had been God.

*

It made the national news. A celebrity involved. Twisted metal strewn beyond the shoulder. Little pine straw fires still simmering. The light fading from the sky as reporters talked to cameramen. A terrible accident, they said. Blue and red lights flashed on webs of yellow caution tape. A helicopter chopped the air overhead.

The details were fuzzy. There was a boy, but measures had been taken to conceal his identity—a minor, you know how it goes. The family planned to release a statement at some point in the future. Probably figuring how to capitalize on the event. Not clear exactly how he fit into the puzzle. There was an incident at the clinic involving the radioman. A nurse had called the police, but they didn't arrive in time. There was a history between the man and the clinic. He wasn't welcome there, to say the least. His motives were unclear. Was he there to support someone? Now that would be a story. Did he know the boy? Was he inebriated? The nurses had already been booked for interviews. Everyone remembered a few years back, but there hadn't been a tox screen yet.

We'll wait for the facts, the reporters said. No need to speculate until we know the facts. Still. The people at the clinic said he was out of his mind. Smashing through the reception window, throwing a chair through the door. There were lots of witnesses. We'll have to wait and see, the newscasters said. Sure, the man was prone to fits of anger. That's why people loved him. And hated him too. Wasn't this reminiscent of a few years back? Just before he entered the treatment facility. We can't speculate, they said. Better wait for the facts. No skid marks on the road, though. Like he fell asleep at the wheel. Which is what the cops would have guessed if not for the clinic. If not for the boy. There was a story there. A familiar voice from the radio, bellowing about father and son. About fire and brimstone. Aborted babies. He claimed he was an angel, the nurse told the dispatcher. There were pieces of him in the trees.

Spring Belle

I'm a huge supporter of women. What I'm not is a supporter of liberalism. Feminism is what I oppose. Feminism has led women astray. I love the women's movement—especially when walking behind it.

Feminism was established so as to allow unattractive women easier access to the mainstream of society.

—Leader of the Opposition Rush Limbaugh

The feminist agenda is not about equal rights for women. It is about a socialist, anti-family political movement that encourages women to leave their husbands, kill their children, practice witchcraft, destroy capitalism and become lesbians.

—Candidate for President of the United States Pat Robertson

Many of the Christian faith have said, "Well that's okay. Contraception is okay." It's not okay. It's a license to do things in a sexual realm that is counter to how things are supposed to be.

—United States Senator and Candidate for President of the United States Rick Santorum

If the Democrats want to insult the women of America by making them believe that they are helpless without Uncle Sugar coming in and providing for them a prescription each month for birth control because they cannot control their libido or their reproductive system without the help of the government, then so be it.

—Governor of Arkansas and Candidate for President of the United States Mike Huckabee

If it's a legitimate rape, the female body has ways to try to shut that whole thing down.

—United States Representative Todd Akin

I struggled with it myself for a long time, but I came to realize, life is a gift from God. And I think even when life begins in that horrible situation of rape that it is something that God intended to happen.

—Treasurer of the State of Indiana and Candidate for United States Senator Richard Mourdock

1.

The girls were late getting out of bed again. Momma walked up the stairs hollering. Girls, she said. Girls. Come on, now, it's time to get up. Into their pink room, polyester curtains, doilies on the nightstand. Pink. Back in the woods, the boy in the red bandana had whispered the word—*pussy*—in her ear.

Give them anything they want. Everything. Come on now, she said, flipping the overhead, her little girls shrieking. No, momma, no. Their heads beneath their pillows. Their feet retracting from her fingers. Curled and cool to the touch. Was this love?

No, they said, no, their eyes pinched closed. Rollie pollies beneath wet rocks in the woods. It was always the same. Every morning, funny for a minute or two. She heard her father's voice. They need to learn responsibility. To fear God, these little Christian girls—from whom? Her husband? Slick customer in a business suit, she thought, staring blankly at the pink folds of the comforter. Where was that boy from the woods? Where her father? Why grow up? Her insides floating away as she stared down at the lumps. Was this the American Dream? Pink. How many women just like her in houses just like hers? Their husbands away in the mornings—off to bring home the bacon. *Malaise*. Her aunt had said that word one summer in the mountains, referring to her mother. Malaise. Her father had been away on another business trip. Business trip, her aunt said, sure.

She tried to piece together how it had happened. Stranded out here in this strange place. She heard her mother's voice. Blossomed into womanhood.

Come on, now, it's time to get up, she said. Knowing they wouldn't listen. Knowing she hadn't listened.

Wondering if she enjoyed this pageantry. She remembered her mother wagging her finger. Staring at her budding breasts. Your brother and father live in this house too, she said. Go cover yourself up.

Strangers now among the look-a-like houses marching through treeless subdivisions. A big house, a family. From mother to daughter. Everything she had ever wished for. Yellow blocks of sunlight falling through the windows.

Now calling out their names, now knowing them awake. Unwilling to rise. A game for them—this life. She heard her mother's voice. Know your place, Martha May. We all have roles to fill.

Listen, she said, bending toward their hidden heads. You have to listen, OK?

Being lenient leads to mischief. Said her mother. Said her father. Idle hands, the devil's playthings. Bobby cut a switch. He never did his chores, was always getting into trouble, running off with friends. Into the woods. Her father whipped him when he came home. Poor brother Bobby. How small the toes in her hands.

She imagined how it had been. Or could have been. Blossoming into young womanhood, her mother said. I looked just like you when I was your age. You'll blossom beautifully Martha May—a flower—have any boy you want, you know. Pretty pink flower. Be careful, though, and walk with Jesus. Be careful of those boys. They only want one thing. Yes ma'am, she answered. Her mother stared at her breasts. Yes ma'am, I'll walk with Jesus.

Imagining the older boys asking her onto the dance floor, smiling. Tapping one another's shoulders—just like in the movies. Can I cut in? Looking for something, her mother warned her. They only want one thing. Pussy, Bobby's friend had whispered in her ear, looking her up and down. Hungry. She had seen that look in her daddy's eyes when he looked at her mother's sister. And even sometimes when he looked at—

Come on, you two, she said. Come on, we're losing daylight here. Pulling the cover off quick. Pale little things laid bare. Song on a pull string. Ma-ma. Ma-ma.

No, they said. Writhing in the light. Give us five more minutes. Please. Their shiny legs unreal beneath the overhead—playthings—she let covers fall.

Five minutes. She walked to her own bedroom down the hallway—her bedroom and her husband's. The pageantry. Five minutes, they knew, always worked.

She was a pushover, she thought, as she checked her makeup in the mirror. Picked out jewelry for the day. Rummaging through the closet, wondering what dress she would wear for daddy when he got home. Dear daddy. They played dress-up in the wet candlelight. After the cocktails and music on the radio, they pretended to be glamorous. Floating for a little while. Out here in the suburbs, pretending life hadn't passed so quickly before the girls came shrieking in.

Lately he had been staying late at work. Just like her own father. Business meetings, he said. What kind of business? She saw long-legged secretaries on spiked heels.

After five minutes, she went back to the pink room. Her Azalea Belles pretending to be asleep. What valiant Prince Charming—Southern Beau mounted horseback—would kiss their lips and take them away from her?

We've got to hurry, she said, or you'll be late. Give an inch they take a yard. Her father's voice again. Shaking his head, nothing ever good enough for him. Never would be. He made Bobby cut a switch and whipped him with it. He stood in her bedroom doorway looking her up and down, disgusted. Faded to late-night business meetings as she blossomed beautifully. Some power bursting from her body. Intangible. He hated how she looked. Just like her mother did. They both blamed her for it. Come on, now, she said. Move it.

When she pulled the blanket off this time, she flung it against the wall, knocking trinkets from the chest of drawers. Plinking to the rug. She paused—imagining her mother hiding at the threshold, trying to catch her doing something wrong. Her daddy in the doorway at night.

Right now, she said, staring down at the soft shapes. Right now. Authoritative. Remembering the creased face of God squinting back at her. Her daddy in the doorway. Not at all like Bobby's friend in the kudzu. Nasty boy, her mother said. She remembered his smile and the red bandana. Striking, gallant. How he whispered in her ear in the green grotto of the kudzu. Pinched the pistil of the honeysuckle blossom. Pulled it through the petals, licked the dew drop away.

They all run away, her mother said.

But momma, said her little girls.

Manipulative. Her mother's voice.

But momma, momma—

No. She plucked them up by their elbows—scrawny—and plopped them onto the floor. Both of them crying already—first thing in the morning. Little Barbara—Barbie—sniffling, her arms crossed in anger. Little Nancy imitating.

No ma'am. Pouting for pity. Not today, missy. Come on.

2.

They went sorting through the heaps of clothes in the dresser drawers. Tiny, sewn together with frills, so cute, for the princesses pink. Little fashionistas turned happy in a heartbeat. Digging through their things. So many things. Momma put a pair of panties on Nancy's head to make her laugh. Always caught herself a little too late.

Barbara put a pair of panties on her own head. OK, momma said, let's stay focused. Barbara hung a pair of panties on momma's ear. Silly.

Always a little too late.

She remembered her father's face. Looking at her. Like a whore, he said. She pulled the panties from her head, put on a serious face.

No, Barbara. Let's stay focused, OK?

But Nancy got to, momma. Nancy got to, and I—

That's enough. We need to hurry, OK?

She looked at her watch, an anniversary gift, golden. Filched from the jewelry box. A plaything for grownups. She still had trouble reading the hands. Her husband hadn't listened. She had wanted something else. She had cried in the candlelight. And daddy bought her flowers. Flowers to fix everything. Azaleas, fading. Her own father, fading. Her Southern Beau rode away on a late-night business call.

When she looked up from her wrist, Barbara was pulling a pair of panties over Nancy's head. Stretching the elastic down hard. Blonde curls sprung through the leg holes. Nancy's neck cricked to the side. Blonde bush peeking from the underwear. Whore, said her daddy. The underwear ripping.

No, she said, reaching out to stop it. No, Barbara. Knocking Nancy down as she pulled the other's hands away. No. Nancy crying on the floor with underwear around face. Barbara crying now too.

What did I tell you? momma said. She flipped Barbie over her knee, and pulled her panties down. No, the girl wailed, kicking her legs. No, momma, I'm sorry.

But it was too late for that. She smacked her bottom with the palm of her hand, and the sound startled her. Again, again. It felt good to hit her. The little legs kicking. Don't fight it, she said. She heard her mother's voice. Don't fight it.

No sense of decorum, her mother said, staring at her breasts. Cover yourself up. No sense of propriety. Out playing grab-ass with those boys in the woods. You have to learn sometime, don't you? Mother teaches daughter, teaches daughter, teaches daughter. Duty to God and husband. Honor thy father and mother. A red handprint spilling. Again, again, again.

Nancy struggled on the floor, trying to get her head free from the underwear. Pink.

She couldn't help how she looked, she told her mother. Then cover yourself up, her mother answered. Bobby cut a switch and wore the stripes like stars. A soldier. She remembered following him through the woods, blindfolded to the boys' fort. The location a secret, holding hands through the dark world, tender, careful. Had she ever even liked the color pink? Her mother dressed her that way. Watch your feet, Bobby said, there's a step here. Be careful, Martha May. This is no place for girls. Slowly beneath the whispering trees, blindfolded like a prisoner, a tomboy. She smelled honeysuckle and mint, wisteria, bursting purple through the woods. She smelled confederate jasmine. The leaves of oak trees rustled above her, pine needles underfoot. Hold still. He pulled his hand from hers. She reached out toward empty air. Hold still for a minute, he said. Bobby's voice behind her, his hands untying the knot. Close your eyes, now. Hands rough on her face, the smell of dirt on him. His voice floating in the dark beside her. OK. Taking his hands away, OK, open up. A tree castle nailed together and sprawling through the green, the kudzu dripping, sunlight sparkling in the twinkle-bright canopy. The hideaway of lost boys, peeking from the turrets, swinging from the branches, wild boys. Ladders and bridges drooping between tree trunks. Never Never Land. Never again. And him in the red bandana. Smiling that pussy smile.

Momma? Barbara was still bent over her knee. Momma, she said. You done now?

You'll know when I'm done, she said, remembering that day in the woods. Seeing red rebels in miniature, stars and bars unfurling. A fort to stop the Yanks, the boys told her. The South will rise again. He stared straight at her—blue eyes—red bandana around his forehead. Her knees went weak. It hadn't been that long ago, had it? He had a face from her father's stories. Great-great-grandparents fighting great-great fights in the greatest of all the great lands. She had felt his eyes—on her skin, inside of her—and knew that she would marry him. Those green-wooded days now gone with the wind.

There was a little nick bleeding on her daughter's spanked cheek. Bright red and dripping. She lost her breath, surprised.

Yes, she said. I'm done. Let me get you a band aid.

Band aid? her daughter echoed. Am I bleeding? She turned in circles with her nightgown lifted up above her waist trying to get a look at herself. Momma did the same thing in the mirror before daddy came home at night. Malaise.

Daughters become wives become mothers. With husbands to please, with children to feed. Her mother told her what would happen if she hung around Bobby's friends. Nasty. They'll stick their fingers up you, she said. They'll put a baby in you.

Nancy leaned naked against the wall, silent. Her pale body rigid. Sensitive girl, pallid. Her flesh frozen in the overhead.

I'll be right back, momma said, wondering if she had hit Barbie too hard. Wondering if they would hold a grudge like she did against her own mother.

She got them dressed quickly. Remembering when nakedness was freedom. Before she began blossoming. She could almost remember. Sliding rock in the summer mountains. Her aunt splashing in the green pool that was so cold it took her breath away. Before her mother started saying, Be careful Martha May. Before she started secreting her body parts away.

Blonde curls, pink blossoms. Compliant now. Pliant. She lifted their arms, and dressed them, talking to herself. A martyr like her mother. What did *martyr* mean?

Malaise. A pink light in a green world where Bobby's friends wanted to stick their fingers in her. Know your place, Martha May.

Their faces were sad in the overhead glare. Fixed. They had always been sad, she thought. She had never taken the time to look.

She flung the blanket above them, and they shrieked as the sky tumbled down. To bump and stumble beneath the pink comforter, now laughing again.

Once upon a time, Bobby let her peek through the cracked door of their parents' bedroom. Lumps in the dark bed. Moaning. He asked her if she wanted to try.

I'll do it one more time, she said. And then we'll finish making it. OK?

OK, the girls said, their eyes upturned as she lifted the blanket. Crouched forms with plastic smiles. She started crying in the pink room. Felt hollow inside, wishing she hadn't hit her daughter.

She remembered those boys in the jungle fort. All eyes on her. Babies from their fingers as they reached up her skirt. Pussy, he whispered in her ear.

3.

After she dropped them off at school, she reminded herself it was a game. That she could keep on driving if she wanted. Start over again. Forget everything her parents ever told her.

Instead, she went to the grocery store. To pick up ingredients for dinner as she did every day. As her own mother had done. She would never be able to leave the children. That's what her mother muttered to herself in the kitchen. A martyr, her father said. But, then again, she could take the girls with her. Bubbly blondes beneath summer suns on beaches far away. Bouncing about in swimsuits, the boys looking at them, smiling, entranced. What was so nasty about that?

She climbed from the minivan with her purse under her arm. Remembering how her mother complained about her father's secretaries. What kind of work in the evenings? she would ask. Awfully long legs on that one. A bit heavy in the chest, I think.

Inside the grocery store, beneath the florescent tube lighting, men undressed her with their eyes. Be careful, Martha May. Sometimes she would let them look. Like a whore, her father said. So what? She swung her hips down the white-tiled runways—antiseptic—bag boys grinning at her down the aisles. Nasty. Let them look. The manager—distracted from tallying pickles—dropped his clipboard on the tile and rushed away.

She remembered her mother talking to herself in the kitchen. Too much skin, she said. Her father vowing to kill Bobby and his friends as he whipped him beneath the basketball hoop.

The cashier rang up an old black man in front of her, and she remembered tall tales about phantoms in the woods. Were her fantasies *prurient*? Her father had used the word. Spooks out for a wilding. *Salacious*? Her mother and aunt whispered about *Mandingoes* and giggled in the mountain house. She remembered Bobby in the hallway at school with his mouth full of soap for saying *nigger* at recess. She had something they wanted, she was told and told again. Keep it secret. She saw white froth bubbling from mouths.

Back home, she listened to the radioman as she chopped ingredients for supper. Immigrants pouring over the border, violent revelations in the holy land, protestors picketing the capital, lawmakers trying—once again—to take their guns away. People wouldn't be able to protect themselves, he said. She heard her father's voice through the speaker. Communist scumbags. The radioman segued into a long segment on abortion and the lucrative sale of dismembered fetuses. Unable to protect themselves. She cried as she peeled potatoes, thinking about her little girls. A holocaust of the innocent, he screamed. A holocaust.

Prayer group on Wednesdays, church on Sundays. A green fort. A yellow beach. A pink room. Three times a week, she went for coffee with another stay-at-home mom. Also named Martha. They talked of children and the world's decay. The world rotting from the inside out. Folks need to keep God in their hearts, they agreed. School committees, play dates, yoga classes, life. Sometimes she and Martha went shopping for things. Things. She always forgot what they had talked about afterward and got lost on the way home. All the streets looked the same.

She read books for Sunday school class and—sometimes—romance novels that she secretly bought with her allowance at the library sale. On the back deck, in the sun, she read and imagined what might have been. That boy in the green swooping down on a vine. A white horse along the water's blue edge.

Her husband didn't love her like he used to, she thought. Her mother had said the same. She never told the other Martha that. Never told her how they had been mad for each other once upon a time. Electric. Hand holding sent shivers, pecked kisses took breath. She used to dream of him, of their life together, a long time ago. What might have been. How they lingered on front porches past curfews. How—after she was crowned queen of the Azalea Belles—he pulled a garter from her thigh with his teeth. How, behind ballooning blue and pink hydrangeas they stole kisses, pretending they were married, Southern Beau and Southern Belle. Now faded at the edges. She heard her mother's voice.

I used to have a body just like yours, she said. I couldn't keep your father off me. She always bragged about how she could still fit into her Azalea Belle gown.

She bought lingerie to wear for her husband. Lingerie from the shopping mall, always feeling awkward. In the bedroom she found herself looking over her shoulder—checking out her backside in the mirror. Like Barbie had that morning. Up on her tiptoes to get a better look.

Vain, her father would say. Whore. He had seen her in her underwear once—dancing in her bedroom. He stood there, thinking she hadn't seen. Hungry looking. Then slammed the door, yelling. Never again. Overeager to fill her plate at supper that night, though. He heaped mashed potatoes next to the pork-chop. Looked like he wanted to ask her something. Like he had been crying. That's too many mashed potatoes, she said. He dropped the plate on the floor. As long as you're under my roof, he yelled, you'll do what I tell you to do.

Sunlight glittered on the hardwood, and sometimes she pretended she lived in her father's old stories. A Southern Belle, pampered, pretty, waited on by everyone. The good old days gone, gone with the wind. How wonderful it must have been. To be waited upon. To be in charge of a house like that. Something to do, at least.

The whole world gone to hell, said the radioman. She played a game where she imagined all the things she could have been. Until it was time to pick up the girls. Baby dolls as Christmas gifts for as long as she could remember.

They'll stick their fingers in you, her mother said. They'll get a baby on you.

4.

When she saw her babies again, something warm spilled over. They talked and talked and talked while she sat flooded in the driver's seat. The world didn't have to end in the cul-de-sac. Somewhere horses streamed over yellow beaches. Green forts tumbled through pinewood and kudzu. She remembered the look on her father's face when he smoked his secret cigarettes.

What did y'all learn today? she asked. They bounced like blossoms in a breeze.

Teacher read a book in class about the thirteen colonies. That's why there's stripes on the flag, Nancy said. She unzipped her backpack and pulled out a tiny flag on a tiny flag post, the finial tip painted gold and pointed. She waved it back and forth. A tiny patriot.

Give me liberty, or give me—

Me too, me too, Barbara said, her little body shaking. As she dug through her own pink backpack.

And fifty stars for fifty states, Nancy said.

Barbie singing, now, to drown her sister out. Fif-ty nif-ty U-ni-ted States.

Nancy joining in. From thirt-teen ori-gi-nal co-lo-nies.

Both of their wrists flicking, syncopated stars and stripes—Shout 'em, scout 'em, tell all about 'em—mirror images mimicking each other. Each shrill voice trying to outdo the other. 'Till one-by-one we've gi-ven a name to—

OK, girls. Momma laughed, eying them in the rearview.

E-very state.

OK.

In the U—S—A. They held out the last syllable until they exploded in giggles. And tomorrow, they said, and tomorrow. Talking over each other, and tomorrow, their little flags dangling in their hands. Tomorrow, we start learning the states.

I was going to tell her, Barbie said.

I guess I'm faster, Nancy answered.

No you're not. Barbie's face turning red.

Yes, I am.

Momma watched the fight unfold. No, you're not. In the rearview. Yes, I am. As if in slow motion. Like she herself was split in two and arguing back and forth.

They slapped and kicked each other first. Then stabbed each other with their flags, their backpacks falling to the floor. Spilling out. She remembered how the older boys at school had always chanted—cat fight, cat fight—whenever two girls went at it. They'll stick their fingers in you. Flock from every fifty nifty. Watching girls spill from clothes. Breasts bouncing, crotches split down the middle, underwear torn from clinched limbs and wrapped tight around pretty faces. The whole world in decay. She heard her mother's voice. Would Bobby and his friends have watched? Those gallant soldier boys? Looked for slipped nipples? Reached for flesh with sweaty hands?

Her aunt had been raped at that cabin in the mountains. She asked her mother what *rape* meant. Shut up, her mother said, and they never went again. Her father's eyes were hungry.

The girls screamed, but she didn't hear them. Just watched them, frame by frame in the rearview. Woman brought about the fall. The good reverend said on Sunday. Know your place. Her father said. Her mother. She watched her children scream and stab one another.

But remained calm in the driver's seat. Until she saw Nancy bleeding. The little flag poles too sharp—golden tips blooming—and Barbie bleeding too. Poked. Penetrated. Blood ran from their eyes.

Stop it, she said. Pulling over, unbuckling herself, jumping into the afternoon. Stop it. Sliding open the door, screaming. Stop it, you two. Fumbling with their buckles, her own hands as clumsy as theirs. A little girl herself. Angry, she tore at them, yanked them from their seats.

Their bodies limp. At the mercy of the world. Her hands pinched around their wrists. Grown to Goliath, two humans hanging from her hands, both crying, their heads rolled back and wailing. Big noises from tiny mouths.

Stop it, she said. Right now. Stop it. You have to know your place.

They stabbed at each other across her body. She saw red. White and blue. She stood with her arms apart, crucified in the shallow ditch. Immense. The whittled sticks digging into her flesh, the girls hanging like ornaments from her hands.

She saw a vision of her father's face in the clouds. Angry, twisted, spitting the word *whore*. She could feel it in her heart. Whore. She couldn't help it. Couldn't handle the noise, and for a moment stood panting, her mind blank. Everything so loud, it was quiet. Her arms beginning to sag. Until—without thinking—she clapped her hands together. Her teeth clenched, furious, swinging with all her might.

Thinking—wait, wait, wait—just before they collided. Wait, wait, wait. But it was too late. Their bodies crashed together and crumpled. Intertwined in a mess as she let them go. Horrified. All the world gone quiet. Like a flipped switch. She stood panting in the heat.

Tangled, they dropped silently into the grass, as she pulled her hands back—afraid of what she'd done. I didn't mean to, she thought. And turned as if to flee. Saw her father's face in the trees. Wait, she thought, wait. Slow down. She turned back and tumbled—off balance—into the green where pink dresses and body parts rolled in the ditch.

She crawled through the thick weeds and caught them. Everything was green and hot. Breathless. A hollow place in the honeysuckle. She smelled grass, gasoline, asphalt, burning beneath the yellow sun. She smothered them to her breast, crying. Rocked back and forth by the roadside with her playthings in her lap. Girls. You're OK, she said. You're OK, you're OK, smoothing their hair. Her fingertips probing tenderly. Afraid to look at them. Her father's face looming. Behind the cracked door.

Now you've done it, Martha May. A flash, then fading, his eyes beating in time with her heart. She hadn't meant to. I'm sorry, she whispered to herself. I can't help it, clutching blonde curls.

Blood and broken skin, slick red upon her hands. Sticky, smeared upon the baby dolls. She dribbled blood on their faces. Little whores waiting for a kiss from Prince Charming. A red tongue and stiff fingers that smelled of dirt.

Bring Bobby back from lost boy years, with friends in flannel grays. To kiss their foreheads, bring to life, and live through antebellum days. She smeared the blood on her face and chest.

Barbie's arm twisted around Nancy's neck, her hand pointed the wrong way on her wrist. Nancy's ear torn off and dangling, her eyeball hanging loose. She looked around to see if anyone had seen. Said sorry again and again. They would need stitching up. Hot glue and staples. She hated them. Flower girls like herself. Loved them. Began to speak to them, then heard her name called through chain-link fences.

Martha May. Her mother in the breeze. Across the green. All the years swallowed at the sound. Martha May, it's supper time. You out there, Martha May? She dropped the baby dolls beneath the chinaberry tree, beside the fire truck minivan. Bobby's old toy. Barbara and Nancy in the roadside ditch, sprawled. Broken. Best friends, her babies, stuffed. In the drainage ditch of the cul-de-sac.

Her momma said she was too old for toys like them. She heard the screen door slapping shut. Momma back inside to wait for Bobby from the fort. She wasn't allowed there anymore. Caught kissing the boy in the red bandana. Nasty boy, her mother said. Asking if he tried to touch her private parts. *Pussy* was the word he used.

Don't take her there again, her father said. Bobby's friends with eyes for her. Bobby too? And daddy? You'll be the belle of the ball, her mother said, all the boys will want you. Sure. She looked down at her bloody arms. Be careful, they always said. Be careful Martha May. Of what?

She picked up her dolls, stuffed them under her arm and grabbed the fire truck minivan from the ditch. The grass cool on her bare feet. Fresh cut, it had that antebellum smell. She had seen framed pictures of plantations, and always dreamed she would live in one. One day. The good old days, her daddy said. The radioman, the good reverend. The good old days. Let me tell you about my great, great grandfather. She walked through the trim yard, through the suburban split-level south, imagining his face in the doorway. The sun on its way down, casting long shadows—lank—through the gloaming. On the petal-limbs of a growing girl, through the yards of the look-a-like homes.

Mermaids in the Floodplain

When the apprentice opened the door to the red dressing room, the woman on her knees turned quickly and wiped her mouth with the back of her hand. A flutter of white satin, then still life. She didn't try to stand up. But instead, sat back on her white high-heels and hung her head like a schoolgirl caught beneath the bleachers. Waiting for chastisement, her blonde hair covering her face, her head and shoulders rounded forward. Later, when he was sitting in the convention hall with all the other young conservatives, the water flowing in rivulets down the concrete floor to the stage, the apprentice would wonder why she had remained so still. *Demure* was the word, abashed, ashamed, her limp forearm glistening from the long slurping swipe, her head just a little lower than the drooping penis of the guru. He couldn't see her face through the veil of her hair, but she looked familiar. The guru's penis was swollen and red. His balled fists plugged into his naked hips like a superhero, his starched white shirt bunched at his waist, his pants in a puddle around his ankles. The apprentice saw it all—the tie thrown over his shoulder, the string of saliva—in the single instant before he jumped backwards out of the room, the guru commanding him, as he disappeared from sight, not to move a muscle.

The boy didn't know if he should pull the door closed and cringed when he heard the old man's voice again. This time it wasn't speaking to him.

Did I tell you to quit, sugar tits?

How different than that famous voice of knowledge that jumpstarted the new conservative movement half a century ago. Cool, calm, collected—even in the face of the hysterical liberals he'd debated on network television. Swallow it, he said behind the door. How different than the voice that praised donors to the institute. The grandfatherly voice that vibrated in the brains of young conservatives as they took the leadership roles for which the institute groomed them.

The apprentice pretended not to listen. To her labored breathing. To the smacking wet gagging sounds. To the guru quietly moaning, quietly muttering. Deeper. But he couldn't help imagining the bobbing blonde head behind the door, the age spotted hands tangled in her hair. Repulsed. Yet aroused on the threshold. He had given up pornography before the summer started, and on more than one occasion had dreamed wet dreams in the institute's dormitory bed.

He remembered watching videos of the guru with his sophomore-year crush. And considered peeking through the crack.

More than a crush, really. His dream girl, the Branch President of the College Conservatives. She had invited him to stay after one of the chapter meetings. For specialized debate training, she said. Alone in the room beneath the student union, they hunched toward the little TV. Feeling alive. He had imagined turning and kissing her, imagined proposing on a beach of white sand. Their future unfolding, their wedding, their first house, their children as they sat in the basement watching old debates. She called him a puppy dog. He imagined her slim body slipping from her clothes as the guru demolished his adversaries in the budding days of political punditry. She was the one who forced him to apply to the institute in the first place. And before the debacle at the campus chapel—and the horrifying aftermath—she had helped him secure funding through the apprenticeship which she herself had held the year before.

What would she have done in this situation? His hand was sweaty on the doorknob.

He imagined her behind the door in nothing but a towel. The towel slipping open.

Soon, another boy came bounding down the stairs at the other end of the hallway. Down the length of the red carpet between the closed white doors on either side, a tan southern boy in a blue suit and bowtie. Bounding right up to the apprentice with a smile on his face.

The apprentice pulled closed the door. Click.

He's busy, he said as the boy in the blue suit reached past him.

Their hands touched, both balmy on the little brass globe.

What do you mean? the boy in the blue suit asked.

I mean he's busy, answered the apprentice.

The other rolled his eyes. They want to take his picture with the notables, he said. The rain's let up for a minute.

He'll be with you momentarily, the apprentice replied.

The boy in the blue suit shrugged. He scratched at his gelled brown hair. It's a shame about this rain, he said, attempting to sound like an adult. I wanted to get down to the beach with these girls. He winked. You know what I mean?

The apprentice nodded his head.

Now they're saying it might flood down there. The whole ocean spilling out. He nudged the apprentice with his elbow. Maybe the girls will strip down and go swimming off their balconies. He laughed.

The apprentice stared him in the face. He tried to make his voice sound like the guru's. He'll be with you momentarily, he said again.

Deflated, the boy in the blue suit shrugged. Whatever, he said, turning back down the hallway. No bounce in his step anymore. Word was, he had hooked up with at least three of the female cohort. Knowing such things, the apprentice knew, would serve his political career. He watched him shuffle toward the stairs. Then up toward the convention hall that had been ringing with rain for six weeks.

Behind the door, he heard whispering and the sound of furniture being moved. Then—all of a sudden—the guru's booming voice as the door flew open.

Just what do you think you saw? the old man shouted into his face.

The apprentice whipped his hand away from the space where he had been holding the doorknob, regrettably focusing on the little bulge in the guru's trousers. Nothing, sir, he said, looking down the empty hallway.

Red and pinched, the guru's face inched closer to his own. Reeking of aftershave.

That's right, the old man said. There was nothing to see, was there?

The apprentice closed his eyes and shook his head. No, sir, he answered.

Come in here, boy. The old man moved aside so the other could enter. He put a hand on the young man's shoulder to usher him into the room.

There was no woman in white satin and no apparent route of escape. A large mirror surrounded by light bulbs sat on the white desk, and in front of the desk was a chrome chair with the old man's gray blazer hanging on its back. The apprentice figured she was hiding under the desk. How childish, he thought.

Listen, the guru said. It's a shame about your friend. No one could have anticipated . . .

He trailed off, and the boy wondered why he had brought her up.

I had high hopes for her, the guru continued, rubbing his chin. Musing on the white panels of the ceiling. Media magnet, he said. A mover and a shaker in the fight for life.

His neck was smeared with bright red lipstick. The same color as the walls of the room.

Might have made a future candidate, he continued. I don't know. She had lobbyist written all over her. He put one fist on his hip so that the apprentice couldn't help but picture him with his pants around his ankles. She always had that doctor politician in her mouth.

What a terrible turn of phrase.

It's the 1770s all over again! the guru shouted in imitation. He shook his head. And the good reverend and the radioman, he said. She had them wrapped around her fingers.

The apprentice nodded. He didn't like the guru talking about her mouth. Or her fingers.

Yes, the guru continued. With time, the radioman might have given her a TV show. She was so pretty. And all of us were on her side, you know.

The boy imagined his old crush on her knees on the carpet, wiping her mouth with the back of her hand.

It's a shame, the guru said. But we must soldier on. That's what she would have wanted.

He waited for the boy to nod.

And you, he said. You stepped right up after that fiasco at the chapel and filled her shoes. He patted the boy's back and chuckled. Probably wanted to fill more than those, he said.

His brass laughter made the boy flinch.

That's why you're by my side, the guru said, clapping him on the back again. Through thick and thin. He looked the boy in the eyes. My best friend in the world.

How sad, the apprentice thought. What was he talking about?

The chair teetered—a little hiccup of motion in his peripheral—but he held his head rigid and concentrated on the guru's mouth.

You already know, the old man continued, this is the most important training these kids will ever get. He looked at himself in the mirror, sucked in his belly, whipped a hankie from his pocket and wiped his neck. I only wish I could get my hands on them sooner, he said.

The boy imagined the old man's hands in a mess of blonde hair.

Raise them from the get-go on the foundational values of this country, the guru continued. Free market economics. The boy whispered the words along with him. And the Constitution of the United States.

That's right. The guru clenched his fists. That's why you're here, boy.

The apprentice nodded, looked to the corners of the room, his eyes sweeping over the makeup table where the chair moved again.

Nothing to see, the guru said, smiling. Everything's A-OK.

The apprentice jerked his head back toward the old man. They need you upstairs for a photo, he blurted.

The guru hitched up his pants, and there again was the damp bulge at the crotch.

How about this rain? the old man asked.

They're talking about floods, the boy answered.

The guru ran his hands through his colorless hair. No matter, he said. We're all right.

The boy thought again about watching the old debates beneath the student union. The old man's hair parted in the same place for half a century. Receding now from the age-speckled forehead. The guru adjusted his tie, and the boy noticed how his skin fell in a fold around the lip of his collar. He wished the guru had done a better job of wiping the lipstick off. There was no real chin to his face, just a polished protrusion in the trunk of flesh. He was as old as the boy's grandpa. Or older. But *virile*, he thought. A word the guru often used to describe the conservative movement.

The men in the pornos he used to watch were always so much older than the women.

Weather fluctuates, the old man said, flinging his jacket over his shoulders like a matador. That's how it works. Weather. Everyone knows that. We'll be all right.

*

Although the convention center was cavernous within, from the outside the building appeared to be a single story of brown brick. It doubled as an enormous bomb shelter, the vast majority of the structure buried underground. The guru himself had helped design it during the height of the Cold War and the communist purge. There was talk back then of a secret safe room for political friends if the nuclear option was invoked. Although the building bore the name of one of the institute's magnanimous donors, everyone just called it the convention center. They always had and always would.

The green lawn that surrounded the building had been underwater for weeks, a shallow lake that prevented the students from taking the promised trip to the beach—a point of high contention for the less studious fraternity brothers and sorority sisters. The beach trip was supposed to be half the fun. A selling point for the College Conservatives who recruited on the guru's behalf. The living quarters—which had recently been revamped to accommodate women—were attached to the convention center by a concrete walkway covered with galvanized steel. This walkway had also been underwater for a few weeks, and most of the young men now followed the lead of the young women in removing their shoes and socks when travelling between the two buildings. Everyone was careful, though, to have their shoes back on before they entered the convention center. Earlier in the week, a barefoot girl was publicly reprimanded for breaking the dress code. One of her friends found her in the bathroom later that day wearing nothing but a filthy smock and scrubbing toilet bowls with a toothbrush. *Discipline* and *decorum* were core tenets of the institute.

Some of the younger instructors had been talking for weeks about the growing sense of cabin fever, about an imminent student rebellion, about a catastrophe on the horizon. But the guru and his closest allies didn't engage in such nonsense. The boys were always pranking one another, and now that there were girls, there were love trysts to deal with as well. Boys will be boys, they said to one another.

And girls, girls, they now added. Nothing had changed. This so-called cabin fever occurred every year.

Outside, the notables—the students who best exemplified the scholastic and moralistic mandates of the institute—perched like sea birds upon the top stair of the convention center's entrance. This was the last bluff of dry land, and the water, lapping upon the concrete, now seemed perilously close to surmounting it. But the session was coming to a close, and no one seemed all that concerned about the water. Crammed into such tight quarters upon this outcrop, the boys in their black and blue suits took every advantage they could to squeeze close to the girls in their bright dresses. Tight dresses. That was the dress code. Bare legs shaved smooth like the ladies on the news networks. The business suits of feminists were anathema here. That too was a lesson learned.

Their ears are in their eyes, the guru liked to say. The overweight girls were put on strict diets and exercise regimens at the institute. Give the folks what they want to see, the guru said, and they'll be more willing to listen.

Everyone guessed that this break from the rain would be brief. The students had not yet tired of watching the photographer splash around in the shallow lake of the lawn. He wore green rubber waders like a duck hunter and moved antically through the water, bringing his knees up to his ears as he travelled back and forth from his half-sunken tripod to the students on the shelf of the stair. He had been trying to get them to twirl their matching red-and-white-striped umbrellas in syncopation, but there was no spirit in their performance. They were too preoccupied with rubbing against one another. Although this hanky-panky was strictly forbidden, the rules were relaxed for the notables.

The instructors stood just inside the glass doors, watching disapprovingly as the boys put their hands on the girls' hips and whispered jokes into their ears. They wanted to get the picture-taking over with and get back to the training which would soon be finished.

Done with this batch, at least, one instructor said to another. The future of the Grand Old Party.

They watched a boy in a red bowtie perform a spinning dance move on the wet concrete and catch a girl in his arms. The photographer encouraged this tomfoolery and soon all the boys had found girls to spin. They all knew the same dances from looking at their phones.

The instructors stared through the glass. How quickly the world changed.

Like a bunch of jigaboos, one man said, and all the others laughed.

When the boy in the blue suit came running back up the stairs, one of them asked him, Where's the old man?

He's busy, the boy answered. Then, noting the frowns of his superiors, he corrected his tone. But he's on his way, sir, he said. He should be up momentarily.

The instructor nodded to dismiss him, and the boy stepped outside to join his friends. The rain began to fall in fat drops once again. The sun was a gray smudge behind the stacked nimbus clouds, and everything smelled of mildew.

What's the rush? another instructor whispered. We're stuck, aren't we? It's not like we can drive anywhere.

We'll get the old man to load us up on his yacht, someone answered. Go deep-sea fishing downtown.

Several of them laughed, loosening up as if taking a cue from the youngsters.

In every picture I've ever seen, said a redheaded man with a mustache, women were sprawled all over that yacht.

Chuckles ran like minnows through the group of men.

Fish in the sea, answered an older instructor, wistfully. Always more fish in the sea.

Outside, the students crowded beneath their umbrellas as the rain began pouring down.

Why are we taking these pictures anyway? said a slick, dark-haired instructor who didn't look much older than the students. I mean, if the press gets a hold of this, he said. If any of these fucking kids post pictures to social media—which you know some of them are going to do—no matter the rules. He threw his hands up. Then we're f—

Watch your language, interrupted a gray-haired elder with gold rings on his fingers.

Everyone fell silent.

And don't forget, the elder continued, you were one of those kids just a few years ago.

I know, senator, the young man answered. I'm sorry about the language. But think about it. He loosened his tie. We're scheduled to continue talking about global warming today. About liberal media bias and the—quote, unquote—facts spewing from the mouths of liberal professors. Right? I mean, that's what we're scheduled to do. And if these kids start posting photos of the flooded yard—well? He threw his hands up. Y'all have seen the forecast just like me. Six weeks and counting. There's more rain scheduled. He shook his head. If they start posting pictures, he said again, the headlines aren't going to say what we want them to say—

There won't be any headlines, the senator interrupted, the very picture of authority. And since when do you worry about what the liberal media has to say?

The younger man steadied himself. I try to worry about what everyone has to say, he answered.

The senator laughed. The others joined in as if on cue. He raised one eyebrow in a dramatic gesture that he had perfected decades ago. Well son, he said, patting the young man on the shoulder, then you have a long row to hoe.

The others erupted, and when the laughter finally wore thin, the redheaded man spoke up again. Climate alarmists be damned, he said. We were talking about pretty little fish! Several men chuckled. Little blonde fish and brunette fish, he said, that'll wiggle up onto a sailor's lap.

The men stared through the pane of glass at the young legs falling from bright dresses.

Wait a minute, someone said as they began to resume their old conversations. Y'all shut up. Here he comes.

They turned quietly in their expensive suits—professional—and watched the guru stride toward them. His apprentice lagging behind, matching his step to the old man's, balancing in the guru's shadow.

*

By the time the notables entered the auditorium—their shoulders and hair dappled with raindrops—the rest of the institute's students were already seated and staring at the stage. They turned to watch the train of gallant future leaders parade down the slope of the aisle to the very front of the auditorium. The guru said pomp should always be maximized to heighten the image. One by one, the notables filed into the front row, concentrating on their posture, their shoulders pulled back, knowing that all eyes were on them. Looks were everything, the guru said.

The instant that the apprentice—the last of them—sat down, a blonde woman in white satin entered, stage left, and waved with a cupped hand at the crowd. A beauty queen. The apprentice gasped as the other students began clapping. He recognized her now. She walked proudly on toothpick legs to the front of the stage and introduced herself.

She was the news anchor of a popular conservative television show, a conservative activist, she said, an advocate for life, a licensed concealed carrier, and a woman, above all, who acted according to her lady smarts—she winked at the crowd—not her lady parts. This was a slogan that the apprentice's old crush had made popular in a viral social media campaign. The students clapped again and some of the boys whooped as the woman did a runway walk to the front of the stage and turned in a flourish like a model. The rain reverberated against the metallic roof like a million machine guns at once.

And that's why, the blonde news anchor said, it is my privilege to introduce to you the most preeminent climate scientist in this country. A man who is no stranger to controversy, a man who holds honorary degrees from a wide array of colleges and universities, a man who has held top positions at some of the most prestigious institutions in our country. A man, she continued, who speaks his mind no matter the partisan politics. Who dares to challenge the status quo, and I believe—

The students began clapping as a small round fellow teetered onto the stage and waddled toward the nearest armchair.

Clearly, he had arrived before his cue, but the news anchor clapped along with the students and took quick little strides on her white high-heels to reach her own chair before the bald man reached his.

The sound of running water accompanied her clicking heels. Water sloshing from the outside in. An odd sound, to be sure. But no one seemed to notice.

This man, she said, holding her arms out to indicate the scientist, is hard at work fighting the climate mafia.

The students cheered louder. In front of his chair, the age-speckled scientist gave the news lady the once over, then snatched her hand and kissed it before lifting it aloft and bowing to the crowd. She was obliged to bow with him. The students went wild, their cheers drowning out the splashing commotion at the back of the convention center where flustered instructors were trying to stanch the water running in from the exit doors.

As the old man sat down, the woman followed suit. She crossed her legs, and her skirt rode up her thighs, leading some of the boys in the audience to whoop again. They elbowed each other in the dark while she adjusted herself. She was beginning to look uncomfortable.

The apprentice found it hard to catch his breath. It was like he had entered a dream. The way the woman tried to cover herself—while in the very spotlight—recalled to him that terrible day at the chapel when his crush had been unmasked. He remembered the cameras snapping and the guardrails giving way, the opposition spilling over the flagstones, the scene splintering into chaos. He thought it had been the beginning of something, but really it had been the end. He remembered her afterward, cradled in the azalea bush babbling nonsense. Everything so violent.

On the lapel of the news anchor's dress, he spied a milky stain. He fled from his chair, trying to hide the bulge in his pants, back up the slope of the auditorium.

Water ran in streams down the aisle to make a little moat around the stage. The apprentice splashed toward the back of the convention center, loosening his tie, untucking his shirt. Everything felt like it was closing in on him. There was too much saliva in his mouth. He couldn't figure out why there was so much water on the floor. He kept thinking the word *wet* and wished his crush was here to tell him what to do. He felt like he needed to cry.

Seated in her armchair on the stage, the svelte woman in white satin had regained her composure. She read from notecards and cleared her throat between almost every sentence. Like something had gone down the wrong pipe. I want people to feel empowered to ask questions, she said. About what they have been fed by the scientific community. It's not making a whole lot of sense when it comes to inconsistent data. Her eyes went wide, and, at the back of the auditorium, the apprentice imagined the guru's cock in her mouth. Same as every porno he'd ever seen. Deeper, the old man had said. He wondered what he might have done to help. She had looked like a little animal on her knees on the carpet. Slopping wet sounds surrounded him now, the water gushing down the aisles. Data, data, data, she continued. Data that has been produced—manufactured—and is being fed to our children—she pointed vaguely into the auditorium. Global warming, she said. Climate change. She raised her eyebrows and wagged her head. Whatever those idiots want to call it.

Several of the students laughed, and the apprentice remembered how his old crush had always insisted that if you could get a crowd laughing, you were already halfway there.

The instructors shoved shoulder bags and briefcases against cracks in the doors. They splashed around in various stages of undress, struggling against the deluge that pulsed more powerfully every second. This was getting out of hand, the apprentice thought. He watched as the water rushed down the aisles toward the stage. The instructors looked like cartoon characters trying to plug a dam with their fingers. He felt very claustrophobic, and watched to see which of the students would notice the water first.

These lies are repeated so often, the news anchor said, that people start saying—oh well, I guess if ninety-seven percent, or whatever bogus number they regurgitate—she stuck her finger in her mouth as if to make herself vomit, and the apprentice remembered the long string of saliva. If ninety-seven percent of all scientists believe that man's activities are creating changes in the weather then—Jeez!—she threw her hands in the air—who am I to question that? But listen to me, she said, getting very serious. Don't question yourself. She swept her finger over the audience. You have every right to make your own decisions.

Several of the instructors had braced themselves against the doors, straining against the silver spray of water bursting from the casings. They looked like figures from catholic iconography. Sunbursts of water gleaming around them. Again, the apprentice remembered the president and that bright day in front of the chapel when all hell broke loose. The photographers capturing that image of her all dressed up like a Muslim. Instantaneous fame. Infamous. That was the beginning of the end. It was their fault she did what she did. The media called her a coward. And what pictures would they take now, in this room filling up with water? He was glad social media was banned at the institute. He heard the guru's malediction. The modern media was the brainchild of leftist politicians. He remembered his crush beneath the poplar tree surrounded by azaleas. Yes, he thought, the media had become an oppressive plug to stop the mouths of conservatives.

And let me tell you—the news anchor leaned forward in her seat—there's a problem when you're led to believe that there's a consensus on global warming. She threw her hands in the air. No sir-eee. Don't believe that for a second.

As she talked, the guru entered, stage left, and bee-lined toward the seated woman. We have to develop our natural resources! she said. We have to—

The guru snatched the microphone from her hand. OK, he said, smiling. I think the kids want to hear the scientist speak.

The children erupted in applause.

Let's give it up for this pretty lady, the guru said, looking her up and down. Full of fire, he continued, pulling on her arm until she rose from her chair. He twisted her in a pirouette. And another. And another. He ran his hands up and down her body. It was egregious, the apprentice thought.

The audience roared, drowning out the splashing of shoes in the first few rows.

The guru handed the very same notecards from which the woman had been reading to the scientist who adjusted his glasses accordingly and squinted at the script. Listen here, the guru said, walking toward the wing. Y'all might hear some commotion, but—trust me—everything's A-OK. By now, the students could hear the heavy sound of water rushing down the aisles and the urgent whispers of the instructors posted at intervals throughout the auditorium. Just stay put, the guru said, and mind your manners now. He exited the stage in a hurry.

The paunchy bald man with the translucent skin and the heavy glasses picked up where the news anchor had left off. We have to develop our natural resources, he said, holding the notecards in front of his faltering eyes. We're talking about reason and common sense here. For America to be great again, we must develop our resources.

A whimpering young lady in the third row stood and splashed across several peers before an instructor physically confronted her and forced her back into her seat. The apprentice thought about all those women crying in the porno clips.

Global warming is a political agenda, the scientist said. The leftists want us to fail!

A few more students stood up and were immediately wrestled down by instructors.

Just stay put, the guru's voice boomed over the speaker system. Everything's A-OK.

That's right, the scientist answered. Everything's A-OK. The simple fact-of-the-matter is that there are unexplained changes in what they call the "climate" all the time. He used his fingers as quotation marks when he said the word *climate*. The "science," he said, has made a sharp turn to the political left. We don't actually know whether the temperature will go up or down in the future. The leftists hate America.

Several backpacks and briefcases went bobbing toward the stage, and one girl near the back—who had escaped from her row—went sliding down the aisle as well. The boys whooped and hollered as she glided past, her dress slipping scandalously up her thighs.

What we *do* know, the scientist said—taking off his glasses, wiping them with his tie, and putting them back on—is that the climate is always changing. And that will never change.

The water sloshed about the waists of the seated notables in the first row, but they kept their attention fixed on the stage, slowly sinking like statues in the flood. They knew they were being watched, so they took a stand to lead their peers. They stayed seated—stoically—their postures decorously impeccable, their eyes fixed upon the stage as the water swallowed them whole. The news anchor was crossing and uncrossing her legs to the delight of the sinking boys. She looked ready to flee at the drop of a hat, but she too knew the rules of decorum. Out in the audience, however, several students crouched atop their seats, while several others made mad dashes up the flooded aisles. Two instructors began brawling with a group of bow-tied boys in knee-deep water, and someone started screaming.

Excuse me, the man on stage shouted. Have a little respect. He cleared his throat and began again. Before man ever had a carbon footprint, he said. Long ago in the days of Genesis. He waved his hands in a vague manner. Way back then—there was climate change.

Just stay put, the guru shouted over the loudspeakers.

Now, all of a sudden, it's manmade? the scientist shouted. Is that what they're trying to say? His face was red. How arrogant! he continued. To think that we—he spread his arms to encompass the swaying auditorium—that we could have that kind of an impact on God's green earth. He stamped his foot on the ground. Great God in heaven, he said.

And as he spread his arms again—Moses-like, to encompass the world—the doors at the back of the auditorium burst asunder and a great wave of dark water gushed into the room.

*

The apprentice climbed an iron ladder to the scaffolding where the light crew worked. His shoes were soaked through, his pants clung to his legs, and the water fluxed below him. Black and green and sucking. Waves swept past in succession, and he lost track of time, unable to process what was happening below. He couldn't stop shaking, and when he tried to stand up, his legs went rubbery beneath him.

He felt like he'd been crawling along for ages when he finally found one of the enormous spotlights and swung it in an arc over the mayhem.

The whole building seemed to be unmoored and heaving. Students swam madly against the tide below him. A tangle of flailing limbs attacking the water, screaming, struggling, drowning one another in their rush to save themselves. He watched one boy bite another in the neck, then scrabble atop the shoulders of two young women. Only to be replaced by another boy who was swinging a metal stick. The girls' arms looked like the frantic tic of metronomes as they sunk, and the apprentice remembered how he had once played the public piano in the student union for his old crush. He tried to shake her image from his head, but he couldn't help remembering how she had sat on the bench beside him and stared at his hands on the keys. In the spotlight, the boy who had pushed the girls underwater was finally washed away by a wave. He was not the only one. *Feeding frenzy* was the phrase that came to mind. Kinked bodies crawling upon the water. Everything muted in the long sigh of alluvion static. Rain pelted the roof overhead.

The apprentice tried not to concentrate on any of the specific violence down below, but—taken as a whole—the slimy mass of movement made him sick. His eyes went glassy, and he saw strange shapes rolling through the liquid. Buoyant elephantine figures washed into the room. The other spotlights—abandoned by their operators—oscillated in the water. Where had they gone? the apprentice wondered. There didn't seem to be any way out. He remembered the news anchor beneath the desk in the guru's dressing room. Down below, the great gray floaters washed—one after the other—onto the stage.

Manatees, the apprentice said out loud. He had never seen them before in real life.

Manatees. Riding the waves from the outside in. Caught now in the circle of his spotlight, one of them went sideways and pinned the scientist against the back wall. The old man called out feebly as the notecards exploded in a puff from his twisted fingers. He popped like a balloon and slumped into the luminous water beneath the mass of the manatee.

There were others, aloof and smooth, moving effortlessly through the chaos.

There must have been drains on either side of the stage because great whirlpools formed and sucked the brown-green water—and everything in the water—toward the front of the auditorium. Students were screaming everywhere, some clinging to debris. And as the water receded from the stage itself, the spotlight paused for a moment on the splayed scientist squashed beneath the gray hulk of the sea cow.

These were animals, the apprentice remembered, that lascivious sailors once mistook for beautiful fish women. He had seen a porno once that was based on *The Little Mermaid*. The old man's busted body leeched bright blood into the wet. And as the water continued receding, the manatee found itself caught. Perched atop this human pedestal, flapping its tail in the air.

Finally, the apprentice found the white-clad news anchor halfway up a stage curtain. Her arms and legs were wrapped around the velvety folds, her whole body resembling a clenched fist. She turned her head over her shoulder as the curtain rotated, and the apprentice followed her eyes to the stage, the dead scientist, the beached manatee.

Tracking the round beam of light from the stage to the rafters, the news lady spotted the apprentice and continued shimmying up the curtain toward the scaffolding. The boy abandoned his light and rushed to help her. But his legs were still rubbery beneath him, and he had to balance between the handrails to hold himself erect. Waves of nausea washed over him as he viewed through the metal grating the snarl of bodies squirming upon the skein of water. He remembered orgies on his computer screen.

He saw someone walk onto the stage. It was the guru. And he was shouting something at the woman in white. He held a pistol in his hand that he fired into the air several times, motioning for the woman to slide down the curtain. The roar of rain against the roof made the gun sound like a toy.

The news anchor's eyes were very wide when she looked at the apprentice above her. The boy grabbed the bunched fabric of the curtain and tried to haul it onto the scaffolding. But the thick folds were much too heavy in his hands. I can't, he cried out to the woman, clenching his teeth and heaving until he fell to his knees. I can't, he cried. I'm sorry.

Down below, the guru holstered his gun and grabbed the bottom of the curtain. He began violently shaking it, the pendant woman spinning round and round until her long legs came loose and scissored through the air.

She was all sinew for a moment, a tense muscle rippling like a flag in a squall.

She looked up at the apprentice. And he remembered again his crush in the azaleas. Then her body went slack. Floated limply free of the bunched fabric, limbs splayed, plunging toward the stage.

It happened in slow motion, and the thud that she made was the first sound that the boy had really heard since the water rushed in. The bright splash of glittering liquid where she landed seemed to hang in the air like the sparkle in a snow globe.

The guru hurried over and crouched down to listen for her breath. Then stood—apparently satisfied—and smiled up at the apprentice. He wagged his finger back and forth and shouted, but the boy couldn't hear what he was saying. The old man lifted the woman's ankles in his hands and began backing across the stage. In the shallow water, her arms floated up above her head. And when her dress caught on a nail, it sloughed off like a snakeskin, turning inside out as she slithered naked from the molting. The apprentice closed his eyes, but he couldn't escape the vision. The scene soggy in his head, her pale breasts bobbing loose in the brown water. He collapsed on the metal lattice and squeezed his head in his hands.

Bodies clogged the whirlpools on either side of the stage, and the water was rising again. When the guru tripped backwards over the beached manatee, he dropped the woman's ankles, pulled his pistol from its holster, and shot the flailing beast in the head three times. Pop. Pop. Pop. Like a cap gun. The manatee's back flipper flapped slower and slower until it stopped altogether above the water. The boy in the rafters watched the old man pick up the woman's feet again and continue across the paludal platform toward the wing. She looked like a worshiper who had been struck senseless by a powerful preacher, her arms trailing a clear streak through the blood and lapping brown.

What glossolalia from the penitent? Disappearing into the shadows behind the lauded prophet. Amid the roar of water and the garbled screams of drowning students. What would his crush have done? There was no precedent, but she always had an answer. He strained to remember her face. Her arm against his arm in the basement meeting room as they watched the old debates. The guru and his cohorts in skinny ties and tight jackets—black and white celluloid—cigarettes hanging from their lips as they made mincemeat of progressives. A different man entirely back then in the good old days. The Grand Old Party. Beneath the student union, they had dreamed themselves into the old recordings. Hot blood ablaze as they argued for the nation's soul. Representatives of the radical right and righteous. The brush of her blonde hair on his neck as she listened to him play piano, swaying gently and humming to the hymn he pounded out. Her clothes on the floor of her dorm room as he stood at the threshold and peeked past her in those final days leading up to the protest at the chapel. He remembered standing in the hallway—as she barred the door in nothing but a towel—peeking past her and wondering what might happen if she invited him in.

The scene below him fell away. The suck of the whirlpools at either side of the stage, the splash of spongy flesh, the screaming. He heard nothing but the rain beating down on the roof above him. Like all the stars falling from the sky.

This will take a while, he thought to himself, hunched all alone on the catwalk, while below him, the water continued gushing into the auditorium. There was no way down. No way out. He wiggled from his slacks, thinking about a woman hiding beneath a make-up table. He wiggled from his white boxer briefs and laid supine on the scaffolding. Cradled in a cage above the flood, he closed his eyes, saw the woman on her knees in the red room, her head bowed, her chest and neck glistening through her hair. Penitent. She was not the news anchor now, but his crush—the golden girl of the youth movement. So pretty, the guru always said. But it was not the guru standing over her. The apprentice felt her precious hair in his fingers. She smiled up at him and batted her lashes. Demure. He lifted her from the floor in a sepia swoon to kiss her parted lips. The beginning of a song. Bump, nuzzle me, manatee. Everything liquid and melting to pulp. They embraced in the room of his mind, filling up with water, her limpid clothes lifted away, and everything luminous beneath. Iconographic as they coiled into each other, arched out the window, a glissade over the sill into fields of sunken cress. Infinite, the green world, they two become one: a naked creature connected and all of a piece, buoyant and flapping slowly through the grassy water, flames on their tongues. He moaned nonsense from the hanging bridge and shivered gray above the dark slosh, the world blue beyond his eyelids. And bright.

The Itch

I have thought of something that's not a part of my speech and worried over whether I should do it. Can we doubt that only a divine providence placed this land, this island of freedom, here as a refuge for all those people in the world who yearn to breathe free?

. . . I'll confess that I've been a little afraid to suggest what I'm going to suggest. I'm more afraid not to. Can we begin our crusade joined together in a moment of silent prayer? God bless America.

—President of the United States Ronald Reagan

The new political philosophy must be defined by us in moral terms, packaged in non-religious language, and propagated throughout the country by our new coalition. When political power is achieved, the moral majority will have the opportunity to re-create this great nation. The leadership, moral philosophy, and workable vehicle are at hand just waiting to be blended and activated. If the moral majority acts, results could well exceed our wildest dreams.

—Co-founder of The Heritage Foundation, FCF, and ALEC, Paul Weyrich

I'm sick and tired of hearing about all of the radicals, and the perverts, and the liberals, and the leftists, and the communists coming out of the closets. It's time for God's people to come out of the closets, out of the churches, and change America.

—Rev. James Robison

. . . We can, and so help us God, we will make America great again.

—President of the United States Ronald Reagan

Well, if they don't know, it's going to be hard to explain. When you turn your heart and life over to Christ, when you accept Christ as the savior, it changes your heart and changes your life. And that's what happened to me.

—President of the United States George W. Bush

I know it when I see it.

—United States Supreme Court Justice
Potter Stewart

The good reverend believed the itching was an act of God. Retribution for succumbing to sin. Perhaps, he thought—pitiful whatever it was—perhaps he would succumb again. He shook his head at himself, weak-willed. That's the type of thinking that brings it about, he thought. A result of the research he'd been doing in his office—research, what he called it—next door to the sanctuary, sprawling. He stared at the computer on his desk.

He had believed he was above it when it started. Proud man. If you think you're standing firm, he had preached to great seas of congregants, you must be careful not to fall. Incredible what these women would do. Anything. Everything. He shook his head again. Hadn't he known?

Outside it was raining cats and dogs, inside the office, dark. He could feel the little tickle begin again. On and off throughout the day. Like worms inside him. They would call it hypocritical if they knew—the media. He rubbed his itchy asshole on the seat of his chair, his face puckered at first, then went slack with relief. What he preached was right. The act was wrong. And so was everything that brought it about. He was not a hypocrite. The pornographic magazines and websites, that godforsaken book by this woman—*they* had gotten him into this.

He stared at the blank computer screen, listening to the rain. Water streamed silver down the stained-glass windows, and he remembered Jimmy Swaggart crying. Predecessor, some would say. And Swaggart begat Bakker and Bakker begat Crouch and Crouch begat Haggard and Haggard begat. No, he would not go that route, twisting in his chair to reach deeper. No one knew. Not yet. Another debate was already scheduled with that woman, and it was high time he practiced what he preached. The itching, though, the itching.

He turned on the computer. Then walked across the room, pretending he hadn't. Masturbation promoter, her only claim to fame. Her book accepted by academics because she was an academic herself. Secular, scientific, a woman no less. Bisexual by her own account. Calm, cool, collected during the debate—spic and span in her business suit, with her short-cropped gray hair and those special glasses that righted her wonk eye. Knocked unconscious by her then-husband in graduate school, she said. Before she left him. She wore it like a badge.

On and on about the rampant abuse of the privileged white males of society. A scourge. Maybe we should wipe them out, the reverend had said on stage. A deft allusion, he thought, to what the radioman had been calling the rise of the feminazis.

Her book only popular because it promoted hedonism. Of course. For everyone, everywhere. Sex, sex, sex. He pictured her naked privates—cropped gray hairs—being passed hand to hand. Squeezed and prodded. Disgusting. Her book called for Sodom and Gomorrah. And on the college campus where the debate had taken place, the educated masses cheered her on—*education*, the word they used. Hell on earth, he told them, when evil is called good and good, evil.

The itching, though, was too much to take. Slimy heads from burrow hole. Itch, scratch, itch. He clenched his cheeks together, watched the rain slide down the colored glass. It reminded him of being a boy, the blurred world on the other side.

The gospel music his momma played after church on Sundays. Greasy smears of acne skin across the windowpane. God's punishment for touching himself. He still remembered praying for forgiveness in his bedroom. Now the same all over again. He made promises to himself, to the Almighty. The power of free will, a fable.

He walked back to his desk and sat down. Research, what he called it. Garbage, filth. The world of that woman's book. It promoted the unpromotable, said the radioman. Touching oneself had always been a sin.

And this research had again allowed that adolescent boy to rear his pimply face. From the old pinup posters to moaning whores with gaping holes. Infinite on the computer screen. God doesn't want us to stand up to sin, he told his congregation. We must flee at the sight of it, turn tail and run. Yet what had he done?

Less than half an hour, half an hour too much. And here he was again. Alone in his office. Seated at his desk with his hand on the mouse. Two weeks after the debate on campus, next week the radio show. The radioman to back him up. Two against one, he thought. He pictured the woman naked—hands and knees on the floor—and frowned. Research.

He leaned to one side on the leather chair as if to pass gas, his curled finger clawing at his rear. Right on the hole, how good it felt. Inside even. Like the slide of water on the windowpane, cool. The harder the better. Be careful, he told himself. His upper body going slack as he eased his buttocks backward onto his finger.

He wondered if that was how it felt for the gays. Easing themselves lax onto each other's stiffness. There was no point to the deed for them, their life a bacchanalia. Penises probing assholes. They would die out if separated from the rest. Put 'em behind fences, said the radioman, drop in food as humanitarians do, and they'd be dead in a few years, no doubt. Good riddance. Sucking and fucking till their hair turned gray and their insides fell out. It was insensitive, of course, but it was true, wasn't it? AIDS had been a sign from God that everyone ignored. He had said so on TV, but what had it mattered? Now there were new drugs for the faggots, covered by government healthcare plans.

She was a smart woman, the academic, the lesbian. Bisexual, anything goes. A shame about her eye, but who was she to question God's ways? Believing herself more righteous than the Almighty. The downfall of all liberal academics: say the same thing twice, three times. Till death do us part. Then what? Their worldview empty, humanity at the tip-top. When pride comes, then comes disgrace. It was the same with people in his own line of work. The televangelists like dominos, all the same. Scandal and money, senate subcommittees, sex. Pride in the wet mouths of flesh. He scratched harder. It was never too late to ask forgiveness.

He sniffed his fingers—rot, death, decay—and typed the website into the search bar. Just to peek, he told himself. A little research. One click undoing all his talk. No. He jumped from his seat and walked to the bathroom down the hallway, gospel music tinkling from the speakers overhead. Private. His secretary away at lunch. Which he had known, he realized, before he turned on the computer. Warm water whispering over his hands. The bar of rose-scented soap brought back from the Holy City when he went to meet the pope last year. He tried to distract himself with memories.

How easy not to do what he knew that he would do.

Back down the hallway fast, as if someone might catch him—to get it over with—a wad of toilet paper peeking from his pocket. Carefully locking the door behind him. He didn't have to do it, he thought, the silver world splattering the stained glass. But, then again, he would be more productive afterward. Then again, it would ease the infernal itch.

He pulled his pants off and folded them. He turned his underwear inside out and placed them on the seat of the chair—the same thing he had done as a boy. Pale thighs, hairless—fat and drooping with age. Headphones from the drawer, the lotion as well, the mouse clicking beneath his rose-scented fingers. Sweaty palms reaching toward his prick.

*

It was worse at night, the itching. Lying in bed beside his wife, the sheets sticky—even beneath the ceiling fan—while she snored beneath the comforter, cozy. Back arched, he rubbed first upon the mattress, like a dog across a carpet, front to back, not enough. His wife turning, muttering nothings from her drooping lips. Lips that used to be pouty. Full, soft, accepting. Would she have ever done the things the women on the computer did? Her eye mask hid bags from hard work. Accountant, partner, lover-no-more.

Then his finger—curled talon of relief. Barely touch at first. Then harder, through the underwear, push it in, leave it there. Two fingers, too much.

He worried he would wake her and escaped over the rug to the terra-cotta bathroom. Looking older each night. Perched upon the toilet bowl, panting, he pushed inside the witch hazel wipes for hemorrhoids. Then pulled them out slowly like a magician. He checked himself afterward in the multi-angled mirror, cheeks pulled apart, looking over his shoulder, absurd, listening for his wife. Clench, then relax, nothing amiss that he could tell. But what could he tell? Like a mouth, the dark abyss, opening, closing, kissing, winking. No protrusions, no blood, no engorged veins. Dirty hair hanging from stained flesh. Posed like those women on the computer screen—hungry—cheeks pulled apart. Wide open. Then plugged.

Bags under his own eyes these last few weeks. Becoming a problem, affecting his work. He touched the inside to be sure, nothing throbbing, how deep? He pushed his finger in—up to the knuckle—and moved it in a circle. Felt his body relax and roll forward. He washed his hands afterward and snuck downstairs to the computer. It was just to help him sleep, he told himself. He wouldn't be able to sleep if he couldn't relax.

Afterward—back in bed—the hum of the ceiling fan was like a woman's breath. He imagined dark angels winging through the rafters above him, their legs, their mouths, all agape. He felt himself getting hard as the itch began to tickle his insides again.

Night by night, day by day pitiful. He used witch hazel wipes, talcum powder, hemorrhoid cream, moisturizer, Vaseline. None of it did any good. Rash invisible, reaching deeper, sex always on his mind. Like he had caught some virus—he cursed the academic—the constant pink tickle, turning red. Until he had to flee to the bathroom to plug himself up. Take a bit of toilet paper with him afterward, toward the computer to do the deed.

*

After church on Sunday—a live sermon taped for a thousand thousand—some of the younger congregants waited for him to finish shaking hands with the people. Among them, the national head of Students For Life, a sweetheart, and her friends. Quiet, patient, penitent, conservative. Grouped along the low-slung brick wall, with wan smiles under the April-gray sky, wearing modest skirts above pale legs, demure girls who were proud to be girls.

They knew a woman's place. Knew there was no shame in it. Tall boys beside them with bowties and loafers, the new look, the new South, the future. Spick and span, ironed creases for the Lord's Day, hairless under there, he thought. All of them slippery. Computers in their pockets, always connected. Fresh and sweet, the land of milk and honey. Suffer the little children to come unto me, and forbid them not: for such is the kingdom of God.

Smart to pick a girl as president, he thought. Deflect a host of attacks. Hard worker too, a golden girl. Sometimes she stopped by his office to talk about the future. Her own, the nation's. A promise ring upon her finger, virgin till her wedding day, daddy's little girl, and a Godly girl she was.

He excused himself from the long line of people and met the youngsters halfway across the yard, shook their hands in the grass. Their smiling faces pointed toward their prophet, their preacher. Hello, Reverend, they said. What a sermon.

Vigorous hands, strong clasps of young men. Young women as well, how the world had changed. Good morning to you, he answered. The young and the faithful, standing here before me, while your peers sleep away their lives. He winked, and they laughed.

Warm outside in the suit and tie. He pulled his jacket off, exposing dark circles of sweat beneath his arms. He'd worked himself up like a revivalist. It always started with a tickle. His face glistened as he smiled. He clenched his cheeks.

We were at the debate, one of the boys said. We thought you did a real good job. The others murmured their assent. You brought her back to the facts again and again, you know, about pornography and sex trading—kiddie porn—the addictive quality. All of it. The others nodded their agreement. She was all, No-No-No, the boy said, his voice high pitched and quick. It's not about that, she said. But it *is*! You told her. That's exactly what it's about. Masturbation, a blight on men. The group nodded, very serious.

You're right, the reverend said, putting a hand on the boy's shoulder. Exactly right. Clench, un-clench, clench. And I wish there were more young folks like y'all who could see through this woman. See what she's actually promoting. He saw the hollow outline of videos loading on computer screens—orifices opening before his eyes. Tickle, tickle. The act itself is wrong, he continued. Lust for the flesh, a sin. He imagined himself behind his desk, watching. But everything surrounding it, he continued, beginning to lose his train of thought. Surrounding the act, I mean—the business of selling sex—is the work of the devil himself. He squirmed in his suit, flesh dancing before his eyes. And remember, he said, shaking his finger, they can't sell it if there's no one buying it. The students nodded their heads.

There's plenty doing that, the president answered. Blonde-headed, blue-eyed, shaking her curls in disapproval. Her own book says so, she said. Looking up at him now, the sweet face of innocence. That's why we wanted to talk to you, she said. He nodded in return, clench, un-clench, clench. We're thinking of starting a protest. Maybe buying up her books from the student stores, or—

She trailed off, her forehead crinkling, concerned. Not burning them, she said. That would make us look like *zealots*. A vocabulary word for her. The good reverend's feet curled. His eyes wandered down the buttons of her dress. Then back up to her eyes as clear as holy water. Unless you think it would be a good idea, she said. He imagined her on her knees, her mouth open. Suffer the little children to come unto me. Suffer me to come into them.

Christ, he thought, shaking his head, his stomach tingling from the itch. All eyes on him while he sweated in the sun. You're right, he answered. They would call you extremists. He wanted to put a hand on her shoulder, let it slip down the front of her dress. Couldn't shake the thought. You need to come with the love of God in your heart, he said. The itch was becoming too much.

Then again, he countered, jerking upright. Maybe a demonstration would bring attention to this trash. His body twisted suddenly to the side. Why don't you come by my office, he said. I've got to run just now. Already walking away, his whole body clenched. It was nice of y'all to stop by.

But, Reverend—

I'm sorry, I've got to go, he said. He threw his hand in the air, shouted over his shoulder. I'll talk to y'all later. Come and see me.

He locked the bathroom door behind him. Dear God, he said to himself, pulling his pants down. Frantic, his hand at his asshole. Taking deep breaths, Dear God, he said, letting out a long whistle. Half laughing at how good his finger felt as he pushed it in. A long exhale, like water on a windowpane. He'd have to get it checked out by a doctor. That finger went in too easy, he thought. Quietly moaning atop the porcelain, ecstatic, his eyes a-droop. He laughed. What kind of sick joke was this? Two fingers in. He was a healer on the national—international—stage, a spiritual guide. But couldn't do a thing for himself. Slap his forehead with his palm, like the old-time preachers. Fall down before the Lord, grace obtained.

This was no joke, he thought again. It was God's punishment for touching himself. Of course. Falling into the trap of that wonk-eyed lesbian, unable now to quit. An adolescent again. He shook his head, his third finger rubbing at the entrance, almost unconsciously. It felt like something was pulling at him. An ache that needed appeasing. Disgusting, he thought, the addiction. The whole mess of it.

That's precisely why that woman's book was so dangerous. Masturbation, a plague. And the eye candy causing it. Rotten. Pulled in—unable to escape. Flesh for flesh's sake. It'll keep you healthy, she had said on stage, and everyone had laughed. But she was serious. Third finger in, loose. Smooth. How hard to quit once you've started. Without the Lord's help, impossible. Curiosity killed the cat and all fools alike, he had answered. Masturbation is a highway to hell. The whole world becomes pornographic. Something really pulling from the inside as he sang sacrifice atop the toilet bowl. Wondering if he could use himself as an example. A martyr to show how to overcome. Or someone like himself, he would have to say. Something really pulling. His mind swept clear.

All of a sudden alarmed. Wait, wait. Like a vacuum. Stomach consuming. From the wrong end. He tried to pull his fingers out, but they were stuck. Dear God. He started playing tug of war with himself. Took deep breaths to calm himself down. It was that woman, he thought. She'd gotten him mad. He tried to concentrate on the gospel music tinkling from the bathroom speakers.

But when he closed his eyes all he saw was the girl with blonde curls. Innocent, he thought. Though something about her face suggested otherwise. A kind of half smile, her lips pouty, like his wife's used to be. Her clear blue eyes looking up at him, unafraid. Her blonde curls bobbing back and forth as she beckoned to him. He felt himself getting hard. Don't do it, he thought. She was peeling off her clothes. And all her friends beside her, young men and women both. Under suits and spring dresses, bald skin, sun-kissed, the pale halos of tan lines glowing. Forbidden. Angels flapping their blonde legs, supple, carnivorous.

He felt the fourth finger at the rim and tried to pull it back. Get out of there, he said. Devil pulling at him. He strained as he pulled, wondering why he had used three fingers at all. The fourth one touching. Could he push it in to make room to pull the others out? Loosen up, he kept whispering to himself.

One way for sure, he thought. Always. To calm down. He took a deep breath and stood up. Thought about how absurd he must look. An old man stepping out of his pants with his fingers up his ass. Like a little boy. Gingerly up onto the toilet seat in his loafers, one, two. Balancing. Squatting there, better for the bowels, they say. Easier movement from the inside—out. Like an animal. He groaned as he squatted.

A pale gargoyle perched, his face twisted in gothic agony as he began jerking off. One hand at his ass, one gripped around his prick. Pressing prostate, pulling penis, what a job. Acrobatic old fool on a porcelain pedestal. He imagined the image gilded—golden—a figurine atop a trophy. Given away by that lesbian academic to the best masturbator of all.

Mask-wearers cheering in the crowd down below, the blonde girl and her friends, nude and supple. He closed his eyes, imagined himself hoisting the trophy aloft. Imagined the college kids swinging in each other's arms as the music began playing, their smooth bodies swooning toward the floor. Touching themselves, touching each other, a spider web of soft caresses. Hands sliding down tight bellies to penises pointed toward the ceiling.

Rocking back and forth on the toilet seat, he imagined tongues twisting on breasts, mouths melting toward crevices, silk legs opening to let everything in. Honey on pink lips, sweet beads of sex. Drool, swallow, gulp, swallow, gag, swallow, swallow me down. Suck me into your skin, baptized in the flesh of the flesh. He saw himself—young again—crouched over the blonde girl, holding his dick in his hands, enormous. Cartoonish. Her legs slick. Go on, she said. The boys grouped in a circle all around them, stroking themselves and each other, telling him to do it. And the girls between them now, rubbing their crotches frantically with the palms of their hands. Fountains of honey. Semen spurting all around.

When he pushed inside of her, she moaned and grasped at the ground to keep from falling through the world. He felt himself spilling over, overflowing, when—knock, knock—he heard someone knocking at the door. Before he could think—sweat-slicked, falling from his perch—he felt the gulp and knew his hand was gone.

Knock, knock. Sir? Toppling from the toilet seat.

You've been in there a long time, sir—I just wanted to check.

Garbled sounds. The reverend trying to find his voice. All curled up inside him now. His whole hand swallowed. Yes, he finally said, I'm fine.

You don't sound fine, his secretary answered. He imagined her ear against the door.

I'm fine, he said again. Then caught himself, controlled his voice. I promise. Everything's fine.

He took tender steps to the mirror, careful not to wiggle his fingers. An awkward image staring back. Naked from the waist down, his arm twisted behind him, his knees out to the sides like a marionette as he stepped closer. His dick still hard below his flabby belly. Who holding the strings to this puppet? I'm fine, he said. His voice hollow as he stared at himself. He didn't want to turn around to look. But he had to.

Bending over, spreading open. Fisting, what they called it, hands duckbilled into buttholes. Disgusting. How the hard-on surviving? he wondered. Feeling very sick to his stomach. Imagining the image posted. The press would have a field day.

Breaking news: the televangelist who led the charge to ban gay marriage in this state has been sighted in a compromising position. To say the least. He claims he had an itch that needed scratching.

Sir, his secretary said. I'm calling your wife. If you need—

Listen, he interrupted—staring at himself in the mirror. Don't you call anyone. His voice was stern. I've had an epiphany in here, and I'm going to write a sermon about it.

Silence from the other side.

You go on home, he said. Come in tomorrow well-rested. Lots of work to do.

But it's Sunday, sir, she said. You have appointments.

No, he answered, not today. Deep breaths to calm himself. I've had an epiphany, he said again. Cancel everything.

But sir—

Just clear the schedule, he said. I've heard a voice on high.

He looked toward the coffered ceiling, listening to her silence. Imagined her on the other side, her hand to her chest, wrestling with herself. Concerned, her face pinched tight beside the door. Would she suck him off if he asked? Jesus Christ, he thought.

OK, she finally said. If you say so. Then, as an afterthought, Are you sure you're all right?

Go on, he said. Tell the kids I said hello. Hubby too, he thought, prim and proper. He imagined her grinding her crotch against his face.

I'll see you tomorrow, she said, her voice trailing down the hallway.

He listened to her go, then picked up his pants and underwear from the floor. A one-armed creature, up on his tiptoes, hooves alighting lightly on the tile. Click-clack. Be careful. A tail peeling out of him, curled up to the shoulder bone.

He cracked the door and peeked out. She was gone. Gospel music from above. Praise be. He walked on his tiptoes like a crab down the hallway, naked from the waist down, erect, a child of God with his hand up his ass.

Teeter-tottering toward his office, he wondered how he would get it out. There was always the one way for sure. He looked at the computer on his desk, his forearm disappearing now. Or so it seemed, inching deeper. Slowly masticated, his wrist gone and more. He could feel his organs squirming inside. Like a child fingering trinkets in an antique store. You break it, you buy it.

He struggled to get the leather guest chair wedged below the doorhandle. The walls of Jericho, fortified. Who would blow the horns? Brass penises jammed down throats. No one knows yet, he assured himself, tiptoeing to his desk. He sat down gingerly on one cheek in front of the computer. Not yet. He pulled the headphones onto his head, squirted lotion into his good hand by pressing his forehead down on the nozzle. Ridiculous. He flicked the lubricant between his legs, rubbed it on the gobbling hole, awkwardly bent to one side and wheezing. It smelled like fish, he thought.

No better than that lesbian, bisexual bitch. Greasy smears on the keyboard. Acne skin, windowpane. Diddling himself from both ends, maniacal. He would have to get it out by himself, he thought, yank it out by the neck. His eyes ravenous, brightly lit. A hunched troglodyte in a dank room, sweating the evil out.

*

An hour later—two hours, three?—he lay curled on the floor, sobbing quietly. His hand still stuck, deeper even, his arm wrenched painfully backward, shoulder down-turned, elbow jerked up at a sharp angle, as if he was being detained by police. Afraid that if he pulled it out now he would tear something inside and bleed to death on the carpet. His own arm become the Lord's sword of fire. Sodomite, Gomorrahn. Lusting after strange flesh. His erection still throbbing, never able to ejaculate. Convinced he was as bad as any faggot that had ever lived. His compassion for himself run out, his excuses, his promises. His anger rising hot in his stomach. As it had so many times in the pulpit. His mind a lash against himself. Imagining the church gone, the TV program, his wife and kids. Laughed off into early retirement. Roaming the hallways of his home alone with his hand up his ass, a crustacean on the ocean floor. Dark. Have to amputate, he thought, let it gobble all the way. Drool, swallow, gulp, swallow, gag, swallow, swallow me down. Plugged up and gasping from the pain.

He believed the knock at the door was his own imagination. Enraptured. How long had it been going on? A voice crying in the wilderness, angelic and sweet. Make straight the path of the Lord. He was ready for death. The voice clear. Blue-eyed, blonde-headed. Tap-tap-tapping again. Good Reverend, it said, it's me. You said to stop by. I saw the sign on the door, but you said—

He was turning inside out, diving arm-first into his asshole. What voice talking to carrion comfort? A flippty-doo, his innards spilling from his mouth. He imagined his organs lumped and leaking on the floor. His twisted skeleton blood be-soaked. Found in his office like an animal in the forest. How would he be remembered? Smote by the Almighty with a thunderbolt of love. Let 'em talk, he thought, as he repented on the rug. Let 'em talk, as he asked for God's forgiveness. Promised to never touch himself again. For as long as he lived, the countdown begun. Dull death pains spreading through his abdomen. Shoulder socket slowly cracking, ribs split apart—from Adam's side, death and woman. Oh, merciful death, he said, come unto me.

Are you hurt? the voice asked. I can't hear what you're saying. I'm calling for help. OK?

*

He was in the hospital for a few weeks. The paramedics paid off by his wife, who was furious at her husband for putting her in such a position. I'm not sure what I saw, one of them said. I don't know how much it would take. How embarrassing. She'd had the Students for Life President ushered away before she saw anything. Little do-gooder doing good. Now she wondered about that girl—what she might be up to with her husband. Sometimes the good reverend talked in his sleep.

There were a host of problems upon his admittance. Priapism—erect for too long. Six, seven hours, who knows? Had to poke a hole in his penis to drain it. Lucky he didn't lose it, they said. Discovered torn walls in the lower colon after surgically removing his hand. Peritonitis. Bloated abdominal cavity, dull death pains spreading. Air pockets and blood. Shoved up and in. How? they wondered, asking her about his proclivities. Wanting lurid details that she swore did not exist. His shoulder dislocated, muscles and ligaments torn, he had several broken ribs to boot. How did he do it?

Induced to sleep, he had visions. Anesthesia dreams. Saw himself in holy tent revivals atop wooden stages, thumping black Bibles with golden lettering. He called out in tortured sleep. In a white suit, his face red and sweaty, twisted beneath the drooping canvas.

Come on, he said. You doggone, sorry excuses for His chill'un. You bullnecked, beetlebrowed, hogjowled, hillbillies. Excess baggage is what you are.

Talking in his sleep. She tried to shush him in the hospital bed.

You dick-jerking, cum-spurting, faggots, come on. You pederasts and ass-lickers and tit-fondlers, you pussy-fingering Philistines. Led to sin by the devil in your pants, come on now into the light. Your wives and daughters spread open for the world while you're off looking for a mouth to suck you down. Gobble, gobble. Sluts and painted prostitutes—lesbian Jezebels lapping at each other. Y'all know who you are. Look at you, holding wide the gateway to hell. Dirty path between your legs, your ass cheeks flapping open. Come on, now, into the light. You young boys masturbating in front of your computer screens, you young women touching yourselves on the other side. Pornographers, all of you, bisexual anything goes, into the arms of King Jesus at the right hand of God the Father Almighty.

Orderlies came to the doorway to watch the show. Elbowed each other and laughed. His wife couldn't have been more humiliated.

I've seen the light, the old man screamed, writhing beneath the bed sheets. Beating the Bible in his dreams. Seen the light and come to witness. So y'all can see it too. His arms outstretched to the tent-top, the sweat pouring down. Baptized in the spirit, he shouted. Stabbed by the sword of the heavenly host. I was lost in the land of Canaan worshiping false gods of the flesh.

But now? he thundered. Now? I'm found. I saw Elijah burning in the clouds. Heard the Lord's voice saying the time is nigh when all the world will be judged with fire. The crowd shouting back at him. Speak it brother. Hallelujah. Praise the Lord. Amen.

I come unto you as a prophet, his eyes ablaze. My insides all cut out, thrusting an imaginary sword into himself, dragging it ragged through his guts. Hell shown to me by fallen angels dancing naked through the night. He swept his arms over the swaying masses. I'm a sinner no more, he said. Slapping the Bible onto the podium, charged with the Holy Spirit.

His wife called out for nurses as he thrashed about in bed.

Behold, he said, pulling from beneath his shirt a colostomy bag, the foul liquid spilling onto the stage. Behold, brandishing the plastic pouch at the crowd, shaking it violently in his hands. This is the world in which we live, he said. The world of the flesh. Pitiful. Running back and forth on the stage. Come on, now, into the light. Come on, you wretched stains. Burst from sex parts, you. And you. He pointed into the crowd. Disgusting. From Adam down, all of us sinners. Come on, he said. Shaking the filth at them. All of you! Up into the light. Deny this temporary housing. For His soul is all consuming. We must repent! For the judgment is at hand. Cast out the demons, burn the body for the soul. He flung the bag up toward the tent-top. For thine is the kingdom, he screamed. And the power. And the glory forever. Amen.

Heavily medicated hallucinations, half dreaming glossolalia whispers, he writhed beneath the sheets until they had to strap him down. He woke up sweat-soaked and confused with nurses all around him.

Nineteen days, then released. Stepping into the bright summer air, leaning on his wife's arm. The rain gone, the radio debate rescheduled with the lesbian academic. More firm than ever in his belief, a new fire burning in his belly. He would put that bitch in her place, he thought. A protest planned at the university, blonde-headed, blue-eyed, fierce. Burn 'em all, he told the student president when she visited the hospital. His mind clear, his eyes set. Burn 'em all.

Back toward his office with purpose, where his computer sat solitary on his desk. Waiting like a gaping hole. Fresh air breathed through the body—His vessel—his heart upraised to the Lord.

Conquistador

White nationalist, white supremacist, Western civilization—how did that language become offensive?

I would ask you to go back through history and figure out where are these contributions that have been made by these other categories of people you are talking about. Where did any other subgroup of people contribute more to civilization?

—United States Representative Steve King

Sometimes we talk about why we're importing so many people in our workforce. It might be for the last thirty-five years, we have aborted more than a million people who would have been in our workforce had we not had the holocaust of liberalized abortion.

—Governor of Arkansas and Candidate for
President of the United States Mike Huckabee

They're not sending their best. . . . They're bringing drugs. They're bringing crime. They're rapists. And some, I assume, are good people.

—United States President Donald Trump

For everyone who's a valedictorian, there's another hundred out there, they weigh one-hundred and thirty pounds and they've got calves the size of cantaloupes because they're hauling seventy-five pounds of marijuana across the desert.

—United States Representative Steve King

Twelve-million illegal immigrants later, we are now living in a nation that is beset by people who are suicidal maniacs and want to kill countless innocent men, women and children around the world.

—United States Senator Fred Thompson

These aren't people. These are animals.

—President of the United States Donald Trump

The citizen woke with a start in a room he had never seen before. Drywall—off-white—perforated with holes, fist-sized. Sunlight slanting through the blinds, broken. Drooping. Must have tied one on last night, he thought. Though his head felt fine as he sat up, the box springs squeaking.

There was a woman on the mattress beside him—turned away. Must be her place, he thought. Black hair tangled down her brown back. Little Mexican muchacha give it up in the late night. Her ass in a thong as he lifted the sheets, careful not to wake her, his eyes adjusting to the light. Good God. He exhaled, wondering if he had sealed the deal. Probably not. Probably whiskey-dicked. Probably still drunk now. He half remembered the bar with the boys. Shots all around. Tequila. What kind of Jimmy Buffet faggots drink tequila at the Rebel Yell? And her? Pretty good for a good ol' boy, he thought. Perhaps they went cruising through Little Mexico afterward. He couldn't remember. It had been a long time since that kind of night. Yo quiero la panocha. He felt like he was floating. He heard mariachi music as he reached toward the woman.

But his hand stopped short, suspended in the cavern of bed sheets, an apparition, while his mind crumpled like a sheet of foil. It was not his arm, this bony brown thing. Gold glitter drooping from the wrist—not his wrist. He jerked back, trying to get away from it, groaning. To shake loose the bracelet and the alien arm that wore it. His vision blurry as he fell from the bed. A conniption fit to the floor—weightless—quick up to his feet. Not his feet. Not himself. Shrunken, he found it hard to balance. Whispered curses in an alien tongue.

Clamping his mouth shut—not his mouth—he tried to blink it away. Feet attached to stick legs—hairy stems—to knee bones and thin thighs in blue and white striped boxer shorts. Billowing on this brown boy's body. Flat belly from the waistband, furry around the bellybutton. Everything tiny and dark.

Frantic from the bedroom—the girl calling out from bed—he moved in flashes down the hallway. She sounded like Martha hollering from the bleachers. Half opened doorways—the trailer long and narrow—people sprawled in death forms beyond. Everywhere. Where? His mind stumbling along. What had happened?

Into the bathroom—yellow—at the hallway's end. Broken tiles underfoot. The smell of piss and something floating in the toilet. A Mexican staring back at him from the mirror above the sink. Mimicking his movements. The whisper of a mustache, peach fuzz on his cheeks. Matted black hair and dark nipples. He felt his stomach turning over. A braided rattail whipping from behind him as he swung his face back and forth.

Grabbing hold of the sink to steady himself, he imagined the naked girl in bed. Did he know her? What made him think of Martha? There were vice-grips pinched onto the metal nubs for knobs. He imagined the sheet falling from her breasts and remembered Martha's voice in the morning. He needed cold water, but when he touched the vice grip, it was huge in his hand, and he backed away, staring at the leggy thing.

His mind misfiring. Thick-liquid-confusion until he finally made it back to the sink and splashed water on his face. It was then that he heard himself moaning. The sounds of a caveman, afraid. Purple spots blinked in his peripheral, and the yellow room swam. Time tumbled down. Breasts with brown nipples swarming. He crescendoed to screaming as the world sped up. A strange noise as he lurched from the mirror. His mind unraveling in cartwheels, he crashed into the walls, trying to catch his breath. Back down the hallway, heads peeking from doorways. Pop, pop, pop.

Black mops of hair. Half-bodies appearing below heads. Half hidden in doorways, arms loose at their sides. Silent. Half-people, come to see the commotion. Bop their heads with a hammer. Slap them back into holes, send them south of the border.

He heard the radioman shouting about caravans oozing north past the river.

He was afraid as he stood wobbling in yellow light. Illegals packed away. Would they cut him out of this beaner boy if they found out who he was? Rapists, murderers. Come north in droves to fuck white women and bask in the welfare state.

The girl stepped from the bedroom at the end of the hallway. Wrapped in a bed sheet, her eyes wide, her shoulders bare. Her knee sliding loose from the sheet—naked—as she stepped toward him, then disappearing again. She moved in slow motion, and his body ached toward that gap in the sheet. Again, she called out. Her hand moved in a vague gesture, and it seemed he had known her forever.

A whore casting spells in the night, his mother had said when he moved in with Martha. That bitch has cast a spell on you. Get out while you still can.

Out. There was no weight to his body. He saw his mother's face smeared along the wall. Closing in, her mouth agape. The half people reached out to grab him. They wiggled against him like teeth. Faster. His screaming pushed him forward. His feet sticky on the linoleum. Faster. Walls of hands snatching at him, he squirmed like a greased pig through the kitchen. He remembered chasing Martha after she showered in the apartment above the grocery store, her flesh slipping through his hands. Remembered playing Pop Warner as a boy. Smear the queer in the field between the playground and the dump.

Through the screen door. Down the steps all at once. He felt like a boy again. Swivel, pivot, juke, jive.

Broken concrete and gravel underfoot, his feet barely touching the ground. A streetlight flickering behind him, the clearing littered with beer cans. Car parts and plastic toys, power tools and scraps of wood. Dogs barked from chain-link cages. Voices trailed behind him. He saw—over his shoulder—the girl in the bed sheet crying in the doorframe. Reaching out with both hands, fingers parted, the bed sheet slipping away. Martha used to flash him in the shopping mall. Her voice was a siren in the empty space. Casting spells. He paused, and she seemed to float into the sky. An angel in the trailer park.

He heard his mother's voice in the tree branches and ran.

No shadows yet. The sky paling at the corners. He ran, bed sheets parting before him in the bush. Tangled to his hip bones in the dust-choked green. Between crooked tree trunks, briars sticking his bare skin, kudzu statues, and nets of honeysuckle. Snarling springtime, heavy with pubic heat. He was a brown tadpole squirting through the green murk. Wondering if he should turn back. He had seen the look on that woman's face before. Martha angry at him. Wanting to protect him. Who did she think he was? Past broken playground equipment and an overturned washing machine. Spray-painted letters on particle board. Toward what?

He slowed down after a while, trying to shake her voice from his head, and listened to his ragged breath. Wiped the sweat from his forehead with the little bone of his forearm. Everything delicate, his feet bloody but his body light upon them. He had watched featherweight boxing matches with Skip, and it was always the Latinos that won. He tried to say something into his hands but was afraid of the voice that came out. After he found his way to the state highway, he realized he wasn't far from home. Not if he had his truck. He took ten deep breaths like the doctor had taught him. Saw little Martha shivering on an orange and yellow paisley couch, reaching out to him with naked arms like the woman in the bed sheet.

Trailer parks sprinkled through the spring countryside, doublewides by themselves farther out. Country folk. Not for long, he thought, setting out for home, past low-slung billboards advertising future shopping malls, past outdoor megastores, movie multiplexes, apartments stretching toward the sky. Developers on their way with visions of suburbia—golf course communities for commuters. At the bar, Terry said he was leaving. Where to?

And who will get the contracts, asked the radioman, as our country continues developing? Immigrants, immigrants, immigrants. While the white man wastes away. City taxes looming, city planning, city government. And who pays for that? Huh? Freeloaders packed into trailers? No, said the radioman. They send their money back to Mexico to build stucco mansions on the beach. They take advantage of the sprawling welfare state, then send their money back home. This is not their home and never will be.

His legs whipped through the grass. Cantaloupe calves. Who said that? The radioman? That doctor running for senate? How many pounds of marijuana had this little body hauled? How much cocaine? How many illegals packed into that house back there? A cancer on the country. Fentanyl-laced opioids. Day laborers moonlighting as drug mules. They got it all worked out.

He willed himself to remember the night before—past the Rebel Yell tequila shots—but he could only picture the girl in the bed sheet. Beneath a halogen lamp in the trailer's doorway, the bed sheet falling away. Her naked brown body ascending. Tequila squirting from her nipples, the whole world turned Mexican in a heartbeat. Worms in bottle bottoms. Waves of them across the border, said the radioman. Honduras, Nicaragua, El Salvador—through the doorway of Mexico. Slinking across the river with tattoos on their faces and assault rifles above their heads. Cartel men laughing to themselves about what they would do to white women.

When the headlights swept over him, he scrambled toward the trees. Jagged black and depthless against the pale blue horizon. A truck rolled up the road, and he watched it, sitting on his heels. The woman was in the pickup's bed, her hair whipping out in long waves as they rolled by. She wailed from her insides, searching for him—whoever she thought he was. And he remembered her whispering to him as she ran her fingers through his hair. No. That was Martha beneath the bleachers. No. His mother in the mountains after granny died.

He had seen news stories of drug traffickers and rapists. Murderers living like kings in federal prison. Deported again and again, they returned en masse. Soon whites would be the minority.

Maybe that girl was pregnant, he thought. The radioman liked to talk about that. Make a baby, you can stay here, baby. Citizen child—your ticket to freeload for life.

He started moving again, darting from tree to tree. Gobbling up jobs, attending college on minority scholarships. Made legal at the snap of fingers. Dreaming the American Dream. They're getting rich off a stolen country, said the radioman. Playing golf and tennis in suburban subdivisions, wearing Panama hats at the country club. We'll all be speaking Spanish soon.

As the headlights came back the other way, he put his fingers in his mouth to feel his tongue. They were a gaudy bunch with their sequined shirts and gelled hair. Women with fat asses in tight jeans. Snakeskin cowboy boots, white Stetson cowboy hats, gold and silver belt buckles to beat the band. He imagined the woman's naked body beneath the sheets. The buttons of her backbone, her hair.

She could have taught him Spanish by pointing to her body parts. Let him taste her skin when he got the answers right. They could have lived happily ever after in milk-and-honey Mexico, chickens, chihuahuas, and children in the yard. He imagined an adobe mansion on a cliff above the ocean. They could have sold bottled beer to sunburnt tourists and led cruises into the Gulf. Could have swum with the dolphins like Martha had always wanted. Drank whiskey from the bottle and plucked guitar at sunset.

Once the truck was gone, he picked up the pace, his stick legs whipping through the grass, the stars disappearing one by one. He weighed nothing at all, sailing upon the wind at dawn. He had learned in school that they were so small because they only ate corn. Squatting in gutters, munching tortillas. He wished he had stayed in bed with her.

At the crest of the hill, he put his hand down his shorts and felt the genitals of a young Mexican man. He tried to imagine the sheet falling away. If he had only kept his eyes closed. Put his cock in. Woken wet from the dream as himself, goddamn it. He was crying as he pulled his hand from his shorts. He started running again along the empty road, the rattail bouncing on his back.

Remembering his own rat tail. His mother braiding it on the front porch before his little league baseball games. He remembered conditioning sessions with the high school team. Back when he still thought he had a chance at the Majors. The world was wide open and girls went wild in the stands.

Eventually he came bounding to the turnoff and felt like a kid coming home. Remembered his grandparents' cabin in the mountains. Up the gravel, past Terry and Ray's trailer, past Doug's—he felt like he could run forever. He could hear the radio crackling through Skip's window. The radioman blasting 24-7. Their trailers weren't much better than the Mexicans'. They had all been forgotten together. White trash and wet backs. Nodding to each other in the mornings, pumping fuel into trucks and lawnmowers, gobbling gas station taquitos from wax paper.

Beer cans in the yard, smoldering ashes in the fire pit. Had someone had a party here without him? He remembered a movie that he had seen as a kid. Two girls switching places at a girl scout camp. Was this Mexican boy now buttoned up in his skin? Hanging out with his friends after the Rebel Yell? He listened to the beeping security system inside, the electric boundaries in the yard invisible. He thought again about the woman in the sheets, the sheets falling off like water, her body floating into the sky. Martha's face in the window of that apartment watching him walk away. He considered going back, abandoning his own life for the Mexican's. Then shook his head at himself. What would the radioman think? This was his home, goddamn it.

Through the beer cans and mower blades, he bounded up the porch steps, jiggled the handle of the door, listening to the alarm. He reached into his pocket for a key. But, of course, there was no key. No pockets on the ballooning boxer shorts.

He heard someone inside.

Then the door fell away: a dark rectangle, suddenly filled with a familiar shape. He saw a vision of himself, squinting down at himself. A green cap and a cutoff shirt. His AR fitted to his shoulder. Heavy, the black barrel staring wide-eyed—cold and metallic.

He called out, his hands up. Wait, he said, wait. Shielding himself, stuttering garbled words. Espera. Escucha. His tongue twisting the wrong way. Wait, he tried to say again. Listen. Imploring himself to drop the weapon.

The white man shaking his head—doppelganger from hell—slapping his brown hands away with the black barrel of the gun. Gold jingling on the Mexican wrist. He watched himself shout, but he couldn't make out the words. Caveman on the precipice of the world.

No, he said. Listen. You don't understand. Louder now, angry at himself. Not himself. Who then, behind the blue eyes? Beneath the green cap? Listen, he said, stamping his foot. What are you doing in there?

But everything tumbled out in Spanish.

Goddamn it. He balled his hands into fists. We have to fix this, he yelled. The shell of his body stumbling drunk from the doorway. Yippee-tied-one-on in a dream.

Listen, he shouted. You—who are me—listen to me. He pointed at himself. His mind began to crumple again, the foil crinkling. He saw his mother in a baseball cap. Saw the woman in the bed sheet behind the door, behind himself, sliding down the hallway, a pale ghost.

He tried to step forward, saying, Listen. Tried to talk to the man and the woman behind him in the bed sheet. What was she doing back there? Tried to apologize. Tried to find a way back—

But the phantom launched into his chest, and everything slowed down at once.

The punch of God. Conquistador smoke. From ancestors down, passed down. Bang-bang. Breath knocked—ka-pow—into thin air. Bang-bang. Kaput. Arrested in speech, the world falling away. Bang-bang-bang. Spinning down a hallway—blurry—he felt his body bounce from the banister, weightless. His mother's face smeared in his peripheral. Bang-bang-bang. Slap them back into holes. Felt fingers in his hair. Slithering down his neck. Shots resounding, felt the blow to his back. Again. Rapid-fire. Pummeled down the stairs into the yard. Bent to the side like a drunk falling left. He couldn't right himself, forever stumbling toward the grass.

Get out, he thought, smelling gun smoke. Get out while you still can. Stars freckled the sky. His mother's freckled face. Freckles on a bare back in bed. Poor Martha. Pinpricks as he slumped toward the earth. Roll over, he thought. Don't give up. His hand groped toward the disappearing stars. His flesh fell away. There were fingers in his hair.

He saw himself, the assault rifle still raised. Staring down, first righteous, then squinting at the other. Confused. Pushing his ball cap away from his forehead. Opening his blue eyes—wider, wider—trying to figure out what he'd done.

The sky dark at the edges. Bright to black. Imploding with his heartbeat. Pa-thump. A bad dream, he told himself. Wake up now. Mumbling someone else's mother tongue. Bleeding out. Mother. Pa-thump. Get out. Weaker still, the shallow breaths hitched in his throat. Pa-thump. Whose throat? Uncatchable, he slumped like a deer that knows it's dead. Slinking out. Wake up, he whispered to the pale sky swirling paisley above him. Martha sprawled on the orange and yellow couch. Please. Tears in his eyes. The bed sheet falling away. Please. Women swooping down like birds. Their fingers—feathers in his hair.

*

She woke up as he jumped from the bed beside her. Sleeping in fits through the morning. Curled beneath the blanket, wondering if he would try to touch her again. Tingle skin, anticipatory. They had only been married a week, only shared the same bed for a week. She had come to live with him from her father's house—another trailer on the lot—a move which her father said she would regret. Puppy love, he said. He cast a spell on you. But soon they would have their own place. That's what he always told her. He was stacking money away.

They were distant cousins through marriage. Come up together with her parents almost a decade ago. Through Texas to Carolina to meet relatives who had disappeared north over the years. Always north. Strangers who hugged and kissed them inside of orange bus stations, in the backrooms of restaurants, on the asphalt of empty parking lots. Everything tastes different in America, her parents had said. But she couldn't tell a difference.

In the trailer that was their new home—tucked into the green foothills—she hugged and kissed him when he cried. When he said he missed his parents. Mother-like, she held him, loved him, told him he must be a man. Make money, she said. Send it home. An echo of fathers and uncles. There was a future to build in this country. A dream they might snatch from the earth.

Cousins, but not really. They went to school like children then worked the afternoons away. She helped her mother clean houses. He went with an uncle to landscape suburban yards. Sometimes she would see him in a neighborhood riding a lawnmower or weed eating. Everything was always so green. There was always work in trimming the excess. America. He wasn't as big as the other men, even as he got older. But he learned to run the machines better than they could. His work was quicker and cleaner, he explained to her. Their uncle nodded along. He would own it all one day, he said. Their uncle patted his back.

In the evenings, he got drunker than the rest because he was smaller than them. Always the butt of jokes, slumping to the ground mumbling nonsense. Until they poked and prodded him and he roared back to life, swinging his fists, furious. Calling for the bottle. Claiming he was America's conquistador. A cardboard beer box on his head as a helmet. The others laughed along. Come to this new land, he said, to make it his. Tearing off his shirt. He flexed his arms and slapped his chest. He claimed he ruled the world. Until someone pushed him over.

Sometimes they left him passed out by the burning pallets, and she brought him home to the trailer where he lived. Leaning through the door, she shouldered him down the hallway to his bed—the same bed they now shared. For a little bit longer, he said. She undressed him and listened to him mumble—then snore—wondering what they would be doing if they had never left. She remembered her mother cooking outdoors and the parrot they kept with the chain around his ankle. He still looked like that little boy who had cried and held her hand on that first long trip across the country. He told her he couldn't remember that trip, but he was glad that she still could.

She hoped sometimes that he would oversleep and get in trouble. Lose his job. Learn a lesson. But he was always right on time.

Sometimes he took her driving in his truck. Chrome rims, the undercarriage glowing neon green, decals of golden lightning bolts zigzagging down the sides. They went bumping through the suburbs, him shouting over the stereo about the company he would own one day. An army of men spinning into the yards atop their riding lawnmowers. An army of men with garden shears and weed eaters, hedge trimmers, leaf blowers marching. Him the conquistador at the head of this army, off into the world laid flat.

He moved quickly through the ranks. Learned to keep the accounts straight. Always working. Or flirting with the high school girls. So cute, they all said, pinching his cheeks. She wondered if she was jealous. Then—a month ago—he kissed her at the rodeo. Told her he loved her as they ate peanuts from a paper bag and watched bulls buck men into the dirt. He had always loved her, he said. And always would. She held his hand. He even had a ring.

He was already managing most of the work accounts, and he scoffed when she mentioned the size of the diamond. Waved his hand as if shooing away a fly. A real tycoon in his white Stetson hat. She leaned into the bony crook of his arm. And they started making plans.

She was almost done with junior college and had a good restaurant job. When she got off work, they would sneak around, kissing in the backseat of his truck. He talked about their future, and she listened. They would move to the suburbs, he said, and live in one of the houses that she used to clean. One with a swimming pool in the backyard and a huge deck strung with party lights. They would pay someone else to do the mowing, she said. Their children would be doctors and lawyers.

Sometimes he woke up at night, but he wasn't really awake. Went sleepwalking into the broken yard. From her father's house, she would see him stumbling over the gravel beneath the streetlamps and rush out to help him back to bed. He mumbled of silver fish in silver water and rose vines on the trellis. Relics from his earliest years south of the border. He cried out to his mother in the moonlight, vowed to make her a queen as she walked him back to his trailer.

That's what she thought had happened when he jumped from bed this morning. Groaning by the bedside, mumbling something, sounding scared. What's the matter? she asked, sitting up.

He screamed like her uncle did last summer when he lost two fingers to the table saw. A red spurt in the blue afternoon. Like a chicken with its head cut off, she had heard someone say.

She was quick from bed, wondering if this is how their marriage would be.

Down the hallway, he made noises like a deaf person. Drunk last night and late to bed from the bar. She thought about their roommates and rushed from the bedroom to shut him up.

He was banging from the bathroom on the other end. Crazed and trying to grab at something. Like he couldn't see straight. Leaning this way—and that—unsteady. People peeking from behind their doors. It was none of their business, she thought. Go back to sleep, she said. All of you, get back.

She shushed her husband, waved him toward her like a child. Please, she said. Come back to bed.

Instead, he took off down the hallway, jerking this way and that, slipping through the hands of his friends.

As she moved toward him, her feet caught beneath the bed sheet, pulling it away, and the men's heads snapped toward her like puppets on a string. Eyes wide. She was furious. These were the men he called *friends*. They fed him shots, bullied him as he stumbled about, waited for him to keel over, then told her she needed a real man.

Clicking their tongues, winking at each other whenever she walked past.

He stumbled into the kitchen.

She shouted at them. Help me. But he was already gone. Help! Flying barefoot across the gravel. Looking back over his shoulder—eyes wide—as she called his name. There were white women in the woods around him, floating through the tupelos, with yellow hair piled atop their heads.

When she blinked, they disappeared.

Come back, she said, holding tight the bed sheet. Come back. Where are you going?

When she climbed into the bed of the pickup truck, she remembered the trip from Texas to Carolina. On the brown plains that squatted beneath the empty sky, they had seen vultures clumped and shrugging their shoulders around the carcass of a cow. They had seen the sweep of slick city lights and pump jacks pecking the earth. He had cried for his mother through the desert. Demanded they take him home. I don't want to go, he kept saying. I have to take care of my mother. Not realizing they were already there. That she was already gone. Holding his hand through the grasslands, she pointed out purple storms on the horizon. Asked her parents to tell them stories about giants and feathered serpents as they slithered up the green slopes of Appalachian spines.

When a Mexican makes a mistake, her father said, he brings shame upon his nation. And so does *she*, her mother answered, looking at her daughter.

The sky was dark and pale above them as they pulled onto the road. Bumping from Little Mexico hidden in the kudzu. Broken asphalt and gravel. A tumble town of trailers and little houses, bakeries, taquerias, tobacco and ice cream stores. Slow down, she shouted, hitting the roof. It was almost morning now. Paler still along the horizon, pale and seeping upward.

She wished she had a flashlight as they rolled down the road, praying they would find him before the police did. Lately, there had been men in black uniforms sweeping the trailer park. Immigration police on the periphery, looking for a reason. The parents of a high school girl she knew had been deported last week along with forty others who worked at the chicken plant.

She yelled into the emptiness that she loved him. No matter what, she said. Please. Come home. Her voice was small on the morning road.

The pine trees looked like paper cutouts. She saw eyes between the trunks. Blonde hair hanging in the limbs. Pale shadows crawling through the grass. She called again, but no one answered.

Beneath the ringing metal bleachers at the rodeo, he had told her he remembered the long ride from Mexico. That he had always lied about forgetting. You combed my hair with your fingers, he said. You held my head in your lap while I cried about my mother. He said he could never forget, that he had only been playing tough. The bulls pounded the dust, the people cheered, the bleachers rang with their feet.

He remembered how she had told him that they would be each other's home. He remembered, he said, saying it back to her, as he toed the earth with his snakeskin boot. They would be each other's home. That's all that mattered now.

In the bed of the pickup, she felt faint, the wind blowing wild her hair. Wake up, she told herself. Wake up. Blown out like a sail in the morning. It was still too dark to see. She shook the hair from her face. No depth to the trees, black paper cutouts, the sun somewhere just beyond the edge. Soon, she thought. Soon I'll see him and bring him him home to sober up. Back and forth along the road, the wind blowing tears from her eyes.

*

The citizen woke to the sound of beeping, a headache birthed in sleep. The alarm system pulsing every few seconds. Like the heart monitor at the hospital. His mother made him sneak her cigarettes. They smoked them out the window, in cahoots. He groaned and rolled to his side, his hand stretching toward a woman that wasn't there. Martha long gone. He groaned, hoping the alarm would stop on its own, remembering the nurse pulling the cigarette from his mother's mouth.

His mind bleary as he pulled the pillow tight over his eyes. Imagining Martha's hands in his hair. Cool fabric on his forehead. He could taste the tequila from last night. Ray, Doug, Terry, all of 'em like a little mariachi band. The bottle jumping around in Skip's hands like a goddamned squirrel. Tequila. He groaned, wishing he hadn't gone. Jimmy Buffet motherfuckers. He remembered a radio in the sand on Myrtle Beach. Martha lounging in a plastic chair, a blood-red daiquiri sweating in her hands. Bopping along to the steel drum calypso music, her hair piled atop her head. They could both put 'em down back then. Beer after beer in the sand. The whole world golden. And Martha weaving between umbrellas in a neon string bikini. I want to look like a Mexican, she used to say, laughing, splashing coconut oil on her skin. Give me all the sunshine in the world. The citizen put his hands down his pants, thinking of slippery dark skin.

Still dark outside—Saturday—probably rabbits in the yard, he thought. Or Skip's dog. Little fucker. The alarm system couldn't tell the difference. Yippee-tied-one-on for sure. His skull seemed to pulse larger with every beep. Larger. He imagined his mother's towering blonde beehive. Larger. Didn't used to get hangovers, he thought. Up all night with the baseball team, go charging onto the field the next day. Yellow days of summer, beach weeks running together like waves. Martha in her bikini bouncing out of the water. Used to wake up drunk and keep on drinking, hair of the dog for life.

That's why his stint at college had only lasted one semester. They took away his scholarship. He heard his mother's voice. You're smarter than that, she said. But she didn't know. Gossiping with the church ladies. Calling Martha a whore.

He wondered if he had a bottle in the kitchen. Drink a drink to his mother. To the good old days. He remembered her in the bleachers. In a red-and-white-striped jersey with his number on the back. And Martha wearing his letter jacket. Both with big blonde hair. Martha in nothing but his letter jacket smoking cigarettes on the paisley couch. The jacket slipping open, her tan lines finger-thin and white as vanilla. He tried to remember the way she put her cigarette out and uncrossed her legs. How she would blow smoke toward the ceiling and smile—

There was something on the steps outside.

Not a dog or a rabbit. Someone scrabbling at the door.

Motherfucker, he said, swinging his legs from the bed. Motherfucker. He remembered Terry saying something about a black boy hanging around the railroad tracks. Motherfucker, Terry said. Creeping along in a hoodie, checking for unlocked doors.

The pounding shrunk to the back of his head, but the floorboards slanted away. He steadied himself against the wall, trying to focus. Trying to find his balance. He grabbed his rifle from the closet. Stumbled from the bedroom.

An obligation, said the radioman. Not a *right* to defend yourself. An *obligation*.

He crept down the hallway, the rifle up against his shoulder, feeling like a militiaman. It's the 1770s all over again. Defender of the country. An obligation. This was his house. His home, impenetrable. The fort of a homesteader, a frontiersman like his great-great-granddaddy. Off into the wild. His mother told him stories. Appalachia frontier. Virgin country, red men. A Cherokee princess bride. Land of the free, home of the brave. He saw her twisted face, cheering from the bleachers. Through the kitchen to the front door, his socks silent on the linoleum. Saw her twisted face in the hospital bed. Never take no shit from no one, she said.

His heart pounding now. Pa-thump. This was it. He had imagined it a thousand times. Home invasion. Bank robbery. Terrorists at the shopping mall. Breathe. He and Skip and Terry down at the shooting range. Breathe. Talking about going off grid. It's the 1770s all over again. No one could say he didn't go down fighting. Pa-thump. His heart boomed in his ears. He steeled himself and took a breath. And angry, clenched his teeth, his house. His home. An obligation. Breathe. His finger on the trigger. His mother's hands upon his head and Martha holding tight. Pa-thump. And angry, he pulled back the door.

Acknowledgments

Ocean State Review: "The Itch";
The Penn Review: "Spring Belle";
Terrain.org: "Mermaids in the Floodplain."

I don't know if this book would have ever been published if Peter Conners hadn't selected it for the BOA Short Fiction Award. When he called with the news, I was at an orientation for a job that was not yet in the bag. It felt suddenly like I had won the lottery, though buying the ticket, of course, had required a ten-year payment plan. Peter's careful reading and thoughtful suggestions have made this collection better than it was. I'm indebted to him and the entire BOA team for believing in this book.

I want to thank my partner Caroline who often makes the impossible possible. My cup runneth over: green pastures, still waters. As a camel, I pass daily through the eye of the needle. Our heavenly kingdom: a tiny old house in little low bottom, too small for a family of four, a lean-to screened-in where we spend three seasons of the year above a backyard jungle beneath the humming interstate. Only by anchoring to you in the most visceral of realities might I take my flights of fancy. Thank you for sharing your life with me, and for teaching me how to listen.

Thanks to my brothers—blood and otherwise—who tell it like it is: Craig, Brew, Fulton. You are at once talking signposts, pointing out unexpected directions, and simultaneously my arm-in-arm companions, skipping off to confront wizards and witches. Novelty inexhaustible: our conversations are a kind of steady unsteadiness on which I choose to dwell.

Thanks to my parents for teaching me to read, for feeding me books, for showing me that the more one reads, the more books there are begging to be read. My mom devoured early drafts of these stories, as she does early drafts of all my writing. My earliest champion, my earliest critic, an eager reader, even if that reading sometimes leaves her disgusted. Thank you, ma. And thank you, pa, for the combative spirit that often gets both of us into trouble. Both of you have always encouraged me to chase that which can't be caught.

I visited the secret Brazenhead Bookstore as a wide-eyed *Bomb Magazine* intern and worked the exhibits and issue launches of Tod Lippy's magnificent *ESOPUS Magazine*. Here were nodes to networks that sprawled beyond the printed page, citizen artists in buzzing hubs of beautifully curated space. Thank you, Tod, Betsy, Michael, for opening my eyes.

Thanks to Chris Tonelli (and the Birds crew) for showing me how literary citizens might move through the world, and to Paul Cunningham for showing me—and inviting me to participate in—the hands-on hard work such citizens must carry out. Thanks to my co-workers at *The Georgia Review* who showed me how literary citizenship might become a career: a profession for which one trains, and which one undertakes as a calling, a field of pursuit in which the pursuers must make their own paths. Thanks to all those writers, artists, and musicians in Athens, Georgia, who pursued those paths alongside me—especially the Kafka boys and the One Night Only Collaborative. From this latter group I owe a special thanks Tim Root who has read these stories and shared with me his bizarre and profane interpretations.

I owe a debt to all the literary journal editors out there. To the few who have published my work, my unending gratitude. And to those who have not, you keep me plugging away.

Thanks to Reg McKnight, LeAnne Howe, and the readers in their workshops who helped me unpack and repack a few of these stories. Beyond the workshops—front porch pipe smoke, coffee on Boulevard, cats prowling the driveway like panthers on Beechwood—my conversations with the two of you have changed how I think about the burdenjoy of writing.

Thanks to Jed Rasula for rewiring my brain, for reminding me that I am always a reader first and that aggressive curiosity (i.e., research) is the heavenly vehicle by which poets might soar through the zodiac of their wit. Thanks to Ed Pavlić who has encouraged me to buck conventions so fundamental that I didn't have the vocabulary to name them.

Many thanks to all my many teachers and especially to those at NC Central who opened the arms of their graduate program to a bartending bookworm and showed him what a real education looks like. Shortly after the entrance interview with the Graduate Coordinator—an interview in which I commented on the framed photos of Meher Baba hanging on the office wall and the polished broadsword leaning in the cinderblock corner—Jim Pearce became the model of mentorship upon which I will always gauge my own efforts. Your friendship, Jim, is wondrous strange, and it will take the rest of my life to pay forward your kindness and rigor.

A special thanks to all my students at Central who are always teaching me at least as much as I am teaching them. Always: more things in heaven and earth: expanding my philosophy. Of course, Otie Bird and Sly are always doing the same. I have no idea what y'all will think of this book when you're old enough to read it, but I hope you'll share your thoughts with me. I've grown old while revising these stories. The youth are encamped on the college campuses again. Revolution, revolution. We might look to them for guidance and courage even as they look to us.

About the Author

Nathan Dixon received his PhD in English literature and creative writing from the University of Georgia. His creative work has appeared in *The Georgia Review*, *The Cincinnati Review*, *Fence*, *Tin House*, *Carolina Quarterly*, *Quarterly West*, *Redivider*, and elsewhere. His critical/academic work has appeared in *MELUS Journal*, *3:AM Magazine*, *Transmotion*, and *Renaissance Papers*. He lives in Durham, NC, with his family and teaches at North Carolina Central University.

BOA Editions, Ltd.
American Reader Series

No. 1 *Christmas at the Four Corners of the Earth*
Prose by Blaise Cendrars
Translated by Bertrand Mathieu

No. 2 *Pig Notes & Dumb Music: Prose on Poetry*
By William Heyen

No. 3 *After-Images: Autobiographical Sketches*
By W. D. Snodgrass

No. 4 *Walking Light: Memoirs and Essays on Poetry*
By Stephen Dunn

No. 5 *To Sound Like Yourself: Essays on Poetry*
By W. D. Snodgrass

No. 6 *You Alone Are Real to Me: Remembering Rainer Maria Rilke*
By Lou Andreas-Salomé

No. 7 *Breaking the Alabaster Jar: Conversations with Li-Young Lee*
Edited by Earl G. Ingersoll

No. 8 *I Carry A Hammer In My Pocket For Occasions Such As These*
By Anthony Tognazzini

No. 9 *Unlucky Lucky Days*
By Daniel Grandbois

No. 10 *Glass Grapes and Other Stories*
By Martha Ronk

No. 11 *Meat Eaters & Plant Eaters*
By Jessica Treat

No. 12 *On the Winding Stair*
By Joanna Howard

No. 13 *Cradle Book*
By Craig Morgan Teicher

No. 14 *In the Time of the Girls*
By Anne Germanacos

No. 15 *This New and Poisonous Air*
By Adam McOmber

No. 16 *To Assume a Pleasing Shape*
By Joseph Salvatore

No. 17 *The Innocent Party*
By Aimee Parkison

No. 18 *Passwords Primeval: 20 American Poets in Their Own Words*
Interviews by Tony Leuzzi

No. 19 *The Era of Not Quite*
By Douglas Watson

No. 20 *The Winged Seed: A Remembrance*
By Li-Young Lee

No. 21 *Jewelry Box: A Collection of Histories*
By Aurelie Sheehan

No. 22 *The Tao of Humiliation*
By Lee Upton

No. 23 *Bridge*
By Robert Thomas

No. 24 *Reptile House*
By Robin McLean

No. 25 *The Education of a Poker Player*
James McManus

No. 26 *Remarkable*
By Dinah Cox

No. 27 *Gravity Changes*
By Zach Powers

No. 28 *My House Gathers Desires*
By Adam McOmber

No. 29 *An Orchard in the Street*
By Reginald Gibbons

No. 30 *The Science of Lost Futures*
By Ryan Habermeyer

No. 31 *Permanent Exhibit*
By Matthew Vollmer

No. 32 *The Rapture Index: A Suburban Bestiary*
By Molly Reid

No. 33 *Joytime Killbox*
By Brian Wood

No. 34 *The OK End of Funny Town*
By Mark Polanzak

No. 35 *The Complete Writings of Art Smith, The Bird Boy of Fort Wayne, Edited by Michael Martone*
By Michael Martone

No. 36 *Alien Stories*
By E.C. Osondu

No. 37 *Among Elms, in Ambush*
By Bruce Weigl

No. 38 *Are We Ever Our Own*
By Gabrielle Lucille Fuentes

No. 39 *The Visibility of Things Long Submerged*
By George Looney

No. 40 *Where Can I Take You When There's Nowhere To Go*
By Joe Baumann

No. 41 *Exile in Guyville*
By Amy Lee Lillard

No. 42 *Black Buffalo Woman*
By Kazim Ali

No. 43 *Radical Red*
By Nathan Dixon

Colophon

BOA Editions, Ltd., a not-for-profit publisher of poetry and other literary works, fosters readership and appreciation of contemporary literature. By identifying, cultivating, and publishing both new and established poets and selecting authors of unique literary talent, BOA brings high-quality literature to the public.

Support for this effort comes from the sale of its publications, grant funding, and private donations.

~

The publication of this book is made possible, in part, by the special support of the following individuals:

Anonymous (x2)
June C. Baker
Angela Bonazinga & Catherine Lewis
Ralph Black & Susan Murphy
Chris Dahl, *in honor of Chuck Hertrick*
Bonnie Garner
James Hale
Peg Heminway
Nora A. Jones
Joe & Dale Klein
Barbara Lovenheim, *in memory of John Lovenheim*
Joe McElveney
Boo Poulin, *in memory of A. Poulin Jr.*
Deborah Ronnen
John H. Schultz
Sue Stewart, *in memory of Steve Raymond*
William Waddell & Linda Rubel